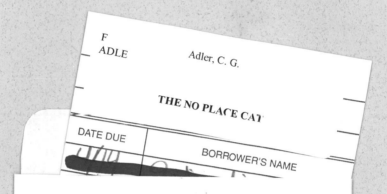

F
ADLE   Adler, C. G.

THE NO PLACE CAT

DATE DUE	BORROWER'S NAME

4/02

The
No Place Cat

ALSO BY C. S. ADLER

That Horse Whiskey!

More Than a Horse

Not Just a Summer Crush

Winning

One Unhappy Horse

The
No Place Cat

C. S. Adler

CLARION BOOKS * NEW YORK

Clarion Books
a Houghton Mifflin Company imprint
215 Park Avenue South, New York, NY 10003
Copyright © 2002 by C. S. Adler

The text was set in 13-point Fournier.

www.houghtonmifflinbooks.com

Printed in the U.S.A.

Library of Congress Cataloging-in-Publication Data
Adler, C. S. (Carole S.)
The no place cat / by C. S. Adler
p. cm.
Summary: Tired of the strict rules and annoying children at her father
and stepmother's house, twelve-year-old Tess walks across Tucson to
her mother's condo, stopping for the night at a state park where she
is adopted by a very special cat.
ISBN 0-618-09644-2
[1. Runaways—Fiction. 2. Cats—Fiction. 3. Family life—Arizona—
Fiction. 4. Stepfamilies—Fiction. 5. Tucson (Ariz.)—Fiction.] I. Title.

PZ7.A26145 Nm 2002
[Fic]—dc21
2001042365

QUM 10 9 8 7 6 5 4 3 2 1

To my Tucson granddaughters, Jenna and Maya,
who share my love of cats and most other delightful things

Chapter 1

After school, Tess trudged uphill to the square tan stucco house where her father now lived with his wife, Blair, and Blair's children. She lagged behind the other kids from her school who were eager to get home. Tess wasn't eager. This wasn't her home. In another month, when baby Sara got old enough to sleep through the night, even the bedroom they'd said was Tess's private place wouldn't be hers anymore. Dad said she had to share it with the baby, his baby, his and Blair's. As if three kids weren't enough for them, they'd produced a fourth between them. Like Dad and Blair were so efficient, they could handle anything.

Even Blair's house looked efficient. The neighbors' had a few weeds growing between the desert landscaping in their front yards, but Blair and Dad let no sprig of green show in their red gravel ground cover. Their specimen cacti were spaced in much too orderly a fashion to resemble real desert landscape. Everything about her stepmother's house was too orderly and neat.

Tess sighed and brushed her long dark curly hair out of her face. Dad wouldn't be home until six, and Blair would be working in her home office, not to be disturbed except in an emergency. All Tess had to deal with was the kids and the babysitter. No problem. She'd just put the finishing touches on her social studies project and then hole up in her bedroom until Dad got home.

It didn't work out that way, though. Tess was heaving the book bag off her back in the tiled entry hall when Brian, the five-year-old menace, sideswiped her on his tricycle. He was always riding it in a circle from the kitchen to the living room, through the halls and back again, although he'd been told a million times not to ride indoors.

Tess yelped in pain and caught his arm. "Your mother wants you to ride out on the driveway, Brian."

"But the babysitter says I gotta stay in the house."

"How come?"

"I woke up baby Sara."

"Well, you banged my leg good just now. You could say you're sorry, at least."

He looked at her bare leg carefully. "No blood," he said.

"So? It hurts and you did it."

"Sorry," he said grudgingly. "But *I* didn't do it to your project. That was Annie."

"What are you talking about?" Tess asked in alarm. She

rushed into the kitchen, where she found her spectacular Egyptian burial chamber lying wrecked on the tiled floor. Someone had knocked it off the counter and ripped it into pieces. Worse, wherever a visible surface was left, it was scrawled all over with red Magic Marker. Annie loved red.

"Oh, no, no, no!" Tess yelled. "I put a hundred hours of work into that model."

Brian snickered. His silly grin made her want to kill him. She couldn't kill wispy, undersized Annie of the big blue eyes. Annie liked to cling to Tess's legs or any part of her body she could latch onto and slobber wet kisses all over her. And Tess couldn't kill the baby, even though she'd like to, because baby Sara kept her awake at night with her crying. But she was only an infant and totally innocent. Yes, strangling Brian was the best option.

Brian must have sensed the focus of her rage because he jumped off his wheels and ran to the bathroom. It had the only door in the house with a lock that couldn't be opened with an ice pick. Tess banged wildly on the door yelling threats. Finally she gave up and went to find the calm-eyed babysitter, whose short hair fizzed up in gray curls around her broad face.

"Annie ruined my school project. She tore it up and wrote all over it," Tess told Mrs. Jackson. The babysitter was rocking Sara in the shade of the ramada, the open porch that ran along the whole back of the house, while Annie sat at her feet, playing her wildlife lotto game. The cool tiled floor of the ramada was littered with Annie's toys everywhere between the gas grill and the padded lounge chairs. Annie was the only one in the family who could get away with messiness.

"That's too bad," Mrs. Jackson said. "When Annie's mother comes out of her office, you can tell her."

"I worked on that project every evening for a month."

"Tsut, tsut, tsut," Mrs. Jackson said with supreme indifference. She wasn't being paid to watch Tess because Dad had agreed twelve was too old to need a daytime babysitter.

"I sorry," Annie said. Her big blue eyes dripped easy tears, and she ran to Tess and lifted her arms to be comforted.

"Don't come near me. I hate you," Tess told her.

Annie wailed.

Mrs. Jackson said, "That's mean, Tess." She picked Annie up and cuddled her. Tess stormed off to her room, deliberately leaving the pieces of the ruined burial chamber on display on the kitchen floor.

Lying on her bed, she brooded about her life. They'd said she'd get used to spending the bulk of her time with Dad and Blair and most weekends with her mother, but a year later Tess still hated it. Nothing had changed since the first time she had seen Blair in the arched doorway of this house with an arm around her freckle-faced boy and a hand holding her cute little girl, like an ad out of some home-beautiful magazine. Those are my enemies, Tess had told herself. They are the aliens who have captured my father, and I shall not like them. It had been eerie to see what a perfectly matched pair Blair and Dad were—both patient, reasonable, bony and nice looking. They wore tan and white well-ironed shorts and shirts and spoke in low tones. Tess's mother, on the other hand, was lively and colorful and yelled when she got angry.

When Dad had asked Tess what she thought of Blair, Tess had said, "She's like my first-grade teacher."

"The one you didn't get along with?"

"Yeah, the one who wouldn't let me go to the bathroom unless I raised my hand to ask."

"Blair is a lovely woman and I'm going to marry her, Tess," Dad had said. The news had hit like a fist in her chest, and the pain had never gone away.

Blair was in the kitchen cooking pasta, Brian and Annie's favorite food, when Tess approached her later. "Did you see my project?" Tess asked.

"Yes, Tess. I'm sorry. I know you worked hard on it and it was beautiful. If you want, I'll write a note about how good it looked and you can take that to your teacher."

"No thanks," Tess said coldly.

Blair bit her lower lip. She said hesitantly, "Well, I picked up the pieces and put them in that box on the counter."

"Annie did it."

"I know. But I'm sure she didn't mean to wreck your project. She's only three and she loves you." Blair's eyes asked for sympathy Annie didn't deserve. What Tess wanted was revenge.

She grabbed the box full of torn pieces of cardboard and paper and cloth and held it out to her stepmother. Blair stood there mutely, as beautifully sleek and slippery as an otter with her boy's haircut and her aggravating calm.

"How could she do this to me if she loves me so much?" Tess asked. She'd been especially proud of the mummies, which were dolls wrapped in gauze bandages. Annie had pulled off the bandages, of course. She always stripped any doll of its clothes immediately, no matter how fancy the costume or how impossible to get it back on again.

Hot tears of frustration spurted from Tess's eyes without warning, and she had to race off to her bedroom to shed them in private before Blair had a chance to respond.

Promptly at six, Dad came home from the computer center where he was a technical support person. Tess pounced on him in the two-car garage next to the kitchen as he got out of his car.

"Dad! Look what Annie did to my project!" She thrust the cardboard box under his nose, only then noticing that it was the same box that had held her old stuffed animals. She had given the animals to Annie and Brian as a goodwill gesture the day she and Dad had moved in with them.

"Oh, wow," Dad said mildly. "Did she really do that?" He rubbed his bald head with his thin, knobby-knuckled hand. There were circles under his eyes from being kept awake nights by baby Sara's crying.

"Yes, she really did," Tess told her only possible advocate. "What are you going to do about it?"

Dad frowned apologetically. "Well, honey, Blair's the one to punish Annie, if that's what you're after."

"Blair won't do anything. She says Annie's a baby. *I'm* the only kid in this family who has to behave right. Everybody else gets away with murder."

"Now, that's not true, Tess. But you *are* the oldest. So—"

"Anyway," Tess interrupted, impatient to get him back on track, "why does Blair have to punish Annie? You said we were all one family now. That makes you Annie's father, doesn't it?"

"Right, but you know that Blair and I agreed we'd each discipline our own children until we all get more comfortable with each other."

"We've had a whole year to get comfortable. Aren't we yet?"

"Well . . ." He rubbed his forehead as if his head ached. "But when Blair asks you to straighten up your room, do you do it?"

Tess knew a trick question when she heard one. Ignoring it, she got to the heart of the matter. "All right. Forget Annie then, but you've got to help me put this back together, Dad. Tonight. Okay?" She had no doubt that he could do it. Her father was good at fixing things. Even Tess's mother granted him that talent. He'd filled up the entire back of Blair's garage with his workbench and hung his tools above it, each one on its own special hook or clamp. Despite herself, Tess was trembling as she waited for him to reassure her.

He peered doubtfully into the box. "Honey, I'm sorry, but there's no way to rebuild this mess."

Tess gasped. He wouldn't even help her! He'd fallen so deeply under Blair's power that his own daughter's needs didn't matter to him anymore.

Before she could accuse him of betrayal, Brian popped into the garage. "Mom says would you come feed the baby. She's got to give Annie a Band-Aid." Through the open garage door came a duet of crying children and ringing phone.

"Yeah, okay, Brian," Dad said. "Tess, we'll talk about this later, okay?" He started for the kitchen.

Tess didn't budge. "Why did you ask for joint custody, Dad?" she asked in a high, strained voice. "It's obviously not because you love me."

"Tess, don't get dramatic on me. I know you worked hard on that project, but—"

She didn't stay to hear more. All hope was gone. Now she would do what she'd thought about often enough during the past year. She put the box down on top of the garbage bin and brushed past Dad in her rush to get to her room. Once there she shut the door behind her and started packing. There were drawbacks about living with her mother full-time—the biggest one being that her mother didn't seem to favor the idea. But she hadn't absolutely said Tess couldn't do it.

Tess loaded her backpack with clothes, her sneakers, her

hairbrush and wallet. She was putting in her sketchpad and some pencils when her father called her to the table for dinner. He and Blair made a big deal about the family sitting down to the evening meal together. He was standing right outside her door, but he knew better than to open it without invitation.

"I'm not hungry," Tess said.

"You'll feel better after you eat something, honey. Listen, I know you're angry with me, but come and eat anyway. Okay?"

"I'm not coming," she said flatly.

Next Blair arrived with Annie. She knocked first, but then she opened the door without permission, as if she had some kind of right. From the open doorway, Blair said, "Annie has something to say to you."

Looking disgustingly angelic, even with the blue star-studded Band-Aid on her nose, Annie repeated the words her mother had undoubtedly coached her to say. "I'm sorry I broke your 'gyp thing."

"I'm not eating dinner with you," Tess said to Blair. "And I don't forgive her."

Annie hid her face in her mother's skirt and whimpered.

"Tess," Blair said. "She didn't mean—"

"My social studies teacher said he'd give me a B instead of a C or a D if I made a really good extra project. He said that would make up for the test I failed. I hate getting a bad mark, especially in my favorite subject."

"I told you I'd be glad to write a note for you. And if that doesn't do it, you can ask him to let you take the test over instead," Blair said.

"No. He wouldn't let me. And anyway, most likely I'd fail it again." Tess had never been good at test taking.

"You'll feel better tomorrow," Blair said. "We'll talk about it then. Meanwhile, please come down and have dinner with us."

"I *said* I wasn't hungry."

Blair shrugged. "Suit yourself, then." She looked around Tess's room, which was in its usual chaos, and bit her lip. She didn't say anything, but Tess knew what her stepmother was thinking. Why couldn't Tess have taken after her sensible, careful father instead of her wild, carefree mother?

As soon as she was alone, Tess finished packing and sat down to write a note to her father.

"I've decided I definitely don't belong with you and Blair, so I'm going to live full-time with Mom. Please don't fuss about it, Dad. You'll see it'll be better this way." She was going to add that she was suffocating in Blair's house, but he was always accusing her of being melodramatic, so she simply signed her name with love and stuck the note in an envelope with "Dad" written on it. She thought the note showed a lot of self-control, considering how badly she'd been treated.

Chapter 2

In the morning Tess raided the kitchen before anyone got up. As she was eating a granola bar, her eye lit on the icky-sweet imitation cross-stitched wall hanging Annie and Brian had given Blair for Christmas. "Home, Sweet Home" it said. Blair had hung the tacky thing next to the window. In a fit of anger, Tess took the red Magic Marker from the pencil holder and drew a big X across the message. Just in case they didn't get the point of her note, she thought with satisfaction.

Tess left the house before anybody else had even made it to the kitchen, as she usually did when she had soccer practice. But today, instead of hiking toward school, she marched down the hill and turned right on the highway. It took about half an hour to drive from Blair's house out to Oracle Road and up north of Oro Valley where Mom's condo was. Tess had no doubt she knew the way, but by the time she'd made the turn onto Oracle, she was walking on automatic, too tired even to think. The jagged brown peaks of the Catalina Mountains had stood motionless alongside her right shoulder for what seemed like ten miles, and she was weary of their constancy. She shifted her overloaded backpack without relieving the ache in her shoulders.

If this hike turned out too much for one day, she told herself, she could camp out overnight in Catalina State Park, which was on the way, and finish her trek tomorrow. Of course, she hadn't brought a sleeping bag, but the nights weren't that cold in Tucson in April.

She was tempted to stop for lunch at a fast-food place in one of the strip malls she was passing. Only suppose somehow the middle school had notified Dad that she hadn't shown up? Worrywart that he was, he could have already called the police to report her missing. It would be stupid to risk being caught after getting this far.

She stopped in the shade of an office building to drink half of one of the two plastic water containers in her backpack and eat an orange. If anyone were out looking for her, a girl with a mop of wavy dark hair hiking alone along the main road would be easy to spot. She poked through her backpack for a disguise. Not even a kerchief, but she found a long-sleeve T-shirt and made that into a kind of hat by tying the sleeves behind her neck. Hunched over a bit, she could probably pass for a homeless person. Besides, if she was lucky, no one would notice she was gone until she didn't get home from school. Annie might cry then, especially if she thought it was her fault that Tess had left, but no doubt Blair would reassure her easily enough.

When Tess started off again, a semi barreled past, scaring her. The full weight of the backpack dragged at her shoulders and for a minute she was lightheaded. It wasn't yet noon, but already the temperature was in the eighties. She just needed to make it as far as the state park before her body gave out. Too bad she couldn't call and ask her mother to pick her up, but Mom would be at work, or traveling around selling cosmetics for her company. Anyway, it would be better for Tess to get there on her own to show how independent she was. That had been one of Dad's big arguments in getting joint custody—that Mom wasn't around enough to supervise Tess properly. Well, she didn't need supervising. She could take care of herself. Even if Mom weren't home much, being alone would be better than being imprisoned in that house full of rules and regulations.

Good thing she'd remembered to bring the key to Mom's condo, Tess thought. She'd move in, unpack, and be sitting there when Mom walked in. "Surprise," Tess would say. "I've come to live with you." And what would Mom say? Tess put one foot in front of the other, imagining her unpredictable mother's response.

Mom might be pleased, "So you couldn't stand having a place for everything and everything in its place?" she might ask and laugh. Or would she frown and argue that it wasn't fair to have Tess crowding her little condo full-time? What if Mom flat out refused? Then what?

"I'm your daughter," Tess would say. "You have to take me in." But somehow Tess doubted her mother would see it as clearly as she did.

Despite the dryness of the desert air, rivulets of sweat ran down Tess's back under the pack. Cars swished past her regularly as she walked along the verge of the road. She thought of hitchhiking, but nobody she knew did that. Even a sweet-looking grandmotherly and grandfatherly pair could be cannibals or kidnappers. Besides, she looked younger than her twelve years. Whoever stopped for her would want to know what she was doing on the road and why she wasn't in school.

Her friend Ria would be surprised to see her on a school day. Ria and she had been the only kids their age in the whole development. They'd been friends forever. Now Tess could see Ria only on weekends when she stayed in Mom's condo, which was a street away from the house that Mom and Dad had owned before the divorce. At least *Ria* would surely be glad to have Tess back full-time. She claimed to have done nothing but watch TV since Tess left.

Tess stopped again to rest after she'd put the last of the strip malls behind her and arrived at where the road was bordered by desert on both sides. She finished off the first container of water. It made a lump in her chest as she gulped it down. The state park wasn't much farther now, she promised herself and made herself get up. Her feet were hot and burning. Her shoulders pulsed with pain. She gritted her teeth and started walking anyway.

What would her social studies teacher say when he heard she'd gone? He liked her because she asked questions in class, like why the ancient Egyptians worshiped cats and what a scarab was. That was why he'd suggested she do the special project to bring up her grade. "I hate to give a C or D to a student as good as you," he'd said when they were talking about why she'd had such a hard time with his big test. The trouble was she only remembered what interested her, and most of the stuff he was trying to teach them hadn't. He would have liked her burial room. He was one teacher who talked to her as if she was a person. "You may not be an honor student, Tess, but you've got a good mind," he'd said.

That was more than her father had ever told her. He always quietly winced at the C's on her report cards, as if they were a personal affront. Once she'd said in her own defense that she couldn't help it if she took after her mother, and he'd said, "What makes you think your mother wasn't a good student?"

The way to get Mom to welcome having her daughter around all the time was to make herself useful somehow. Like how? Maybe she could take over doing the wash. Despite the fact that Mom bought herself fancy clothes that needed special handling, she hated having to separate dark clothes from light, and hand-wash silks, and spray spot remover on whatever needed it before dumping a blouse or skirt into the machine. Those were all things Blair did. The only task Blair had assigned to Tess was straightening up her own bedroom. That was so pointless that Tess had resisted doing it until they finally let her keep her door closed and live however she wanted behind it.

Blair had frowned with irritation at that "compromise." One point for me, Tess had thought gleefully when she'd heard Blair complaining to Dad about it. Not nice, Tess told herself. "You're not nice." Well, she'd never denied her faults. Anyway, Dad reminded her of them often enough.

"Tess, you are rude. You are overly emotional. And why do you have to be so nasty?"

Come to think of it, she *had* been sort of nasty to Annie. And wrecking Blair's wall hanging had been mean. Too bad, Tess told herself. If she ever got over being mad about the destruction of the burial chamber, she'd make up with Annie. At least *Annie* loved her. Maybe she was the only one who really did.

Tess reached Catalina State Park hours before dark, in plenty of time to find a spot to hole up for the night. To get to where she remembered camping with Dad, she had to cross a wide, shallow stream. Its chilly water came from snowmelt on the surrounding mountains, and Tess couldn't wait to cool her sore feet in it. She sat down and pulled off her hiking boots and socks.

She was wiggling her toes in the water when she saw the

cat. It had emerged from a clump of high grass alongside the stream a few feet away from her. Now it sat, swishing its tail back and forth from one haunch to the other. Green eyes regarded Tess steadily from a round gray-striped face above a white bib of a chest.

"Hi," Tess said. "What are you doing here? Hunting for supper?" If so, the cat had ranged far from wherever it lived, because the state park was miles from any private homes.

The cat yawned, showing sharp little teeth and a bright pink tongue. It looked too domestic to last long in this wilderness. A coyote would snap it up for an appetizer if the cat were still roaming around after dark.

"So, you hungry?" Tess dug out the cold cooked hot dog she'd intended for her supper and broke off a piece of it. "Here." She held out the meat. The cat looked at it and dipped its head to clean its shoulder with its tongue.

"Are you lost, Cat?" she asked. "Do you belong to someone in the campground?" She reached out her hand, but the cat drew back.

"Hey, you don't have to be scared of me," Tess said. "I'm on the lam, too." In case it was really hungry and too shy to approach her, she threw the piece of hot dog close to it. The cat sniffed the meat, then rolled it casually under its nose with a disdainful paw. Another sniff, and the cat ate the meat as if it were too polite to refuse, whether it needed a handout or not. The pink tongue slipped out and curled to the left and right of its mouth. Neater than using a napkin, Tess thought. The green eyes were now gravely studying Tess's face.

"Well, so long and good luck," she said. She stood up, gathered her belongings, and waded out into the shallow water. Near the shore it was a little rocky underfoot, but then the bottom turned sandy and the icy water and soft sand felt as good as she'd expected. On the other side of the stream, Tess looked back. The cat was standing watching her.

"Meow?" it questioned.

"Sorry," Tess said. "I need to eat the rest of the hot dog myself. You'll have to catch your own meal."

The cat rose and stretched toward the stream. Then it walked along the bank a few feet and took a small leap onto the first of a series of uneven rocks that threaded a path across the stream from one bank to another. Tess was surprised. She had thought that cats avoided water. This one actually was risking a wetting to get across. Cautiously it climbed and jumped from one rock to another until it had reached the side where she stood. What happened next surprised her even more. The cat stepped right up to her and sat back on its haunches again.

"Well, you are a strange one," Tess said. She was tempted to share more of her supper, but she decided not to let the cat think that she could continue to feed it. This was no time to be adopting a pet. More to the point, her mother hated cats.

"Listen," Tess told it. "You'd better go where you belong." Unless it didn't belong anywhere. Unless the cat, like her, had no place to call home.

Chapter 3

The mountains were reddening in the evening light as Tess headed up the hill for the campground to find some kind of shelter for the night. She lugged her backpack wearily past a tree-size saguaro crowned with an early bloom of white flowers. A woodpecker with a red chin disappeared into a hole above the saguaro's six thick green arms.

She came to the turnoff for the Romero Pools trail. How impressed Dad had been with her when she'd hiked that whole trail with him a year and a half ago! She'd felt proud to be the companion to him that her mother had refused to be. It had only been on their way down that he'd told her that he and Mom were getting divorced.

Suddenly the canyon's beautiful wind and water-carved boulders had changed into menacing gargoyles for Tess. "You don't love each other anymore?" she had asked.

"It's more that your mother doesn't feel like being married anymore," he'd said.

Tess had asked if it was her fault, and he'd said, "No," that they both loved her a lot and were glad they'd had her, but that her mother wanted to be free to come and go as she pleased.

Tess had suggested that Mom might change her mind. "She does that a lot, you know."

"Not this time," Dad had assured her. And he'd said that her mother was bored with him because he liked routines and she liked excitement. "We're too different from each other," he'd said.

"Then why did you get married?"

"Probably we shouldn't have."

And Tess had thought that they also shouldn't have had her. The hike had been ruined for her, just as her life had been ruined because her parents didn't fit together and she didn't fit with them.

Tess glanced back to find the cat still following her up the hill. "Do you belong in the campground?" she asked it. "Are you going back to your family now?" She stopped to rest on a flat rock. The relief in her shoulders was immediate as the rock took the weight of the backpack.

"Too bad you're not a dog," she told the cat. "Then you could help me lug my stuff. Dogs are useful. Cats just sit around looking pretty."

If the cat understood her, it didn't take offense. In fact, it now pretended interest in a lizard that had disappeared under a prickly pear. After a while Tess hefted the back-pack onto her aching shoulders and began climbing again. The cat strolled behind her, maintaining an arm's length distance. Tess's neck and arms and shoulders burned.

She stopped to dump out her jeans and sneakers and whatever else would lighten the load.

"That your cat?" a hiker in baggy shorts asked as she and her elderly companion passed by with their walking sticks and floppy hats and fanny packs.

"No, is it yours?" Tess asked.

The woman laughed as if she'd made a joke. In a minute she was out of sight down the hill.

The pack didn't seem any lighter without the jeans and sneakers, so Tess put them back in and moved on. The campground was in a grove of pine trees. The sites where people set up their tents or parked their campers were far enough apart to allow some privacy. Not many were occupied on a weekday in April, but smoke rose from a grill on a metal post at a site near the entrance. Tess approached the man and boy building a fire there and asked politely, "Could I leave my backpack with you for a while? I have to look for someone and it's kind of hard to lug it around."

"No problem," the man said. He continued busily poking at the charcoal.

"That your cat?" the boy, whom Tess guessed to be about ten, asked.

"No," she said. "I'm looking for its owner."

"It acts like it's yours," the boy said.

"That's because I fed it some of my supper."

"Oh, yeah?" the boy said. "Dad, can I give it some of our hamburger meat?"

"Some," the father said. "But you can't take it home with us even if it decides to follow you instead of her."

The boy shrugged and went to a plastic cooler. Meanwhile, Tess continued exploring. Even without the pack, she was so tired all she wanted was to find a place where she could lie down. The campground stretched out forever. By the time she'd asked half a dozen people if they'd lost a cat, she wasn't sure how to get back to where she'd left her belongings.

The cat wasn't following her anymore. No matter, Tess told herself. It probably preferred hamburger to hot dogs. Fine with her if it stayed with the boy. But where was *she* going to stay? She couldn't very well ask if she could share somebody's tent. They'd think she was crazy. Or else they'd figure she was a runaway. One cell-phone call and she'd be bounced back to her father tonight.

The woodsy smell of grilled meat made her salivate as she passed picnic tables where people were eating. She was hungry. She was thirsty. But most of all she was pooped. By the time she found the father-son campsite again, it was evening. The sky was still light, but the ground was darkening around her. Her pack and plastic food bag were where she'd left them, but nobody was around. Not even the cat. The father and his son must have gone home, she realized—finished their last meal at the campground and left.

After she had dined on the meat and half the fruit and granola in the food bag, she decided that sleeping here alone without a tent or sleeping bag would look suspicious. She'd better hide herself in the lush undergrowth back down the hill near the river and closer to the parking lot, where there were portable toilets and water. The temperature had dropped twenty degrees or more, as it always did at night in the desert. She unstrapped her backpack and took out a sweatshirt, a sweater, and the second pair of jeans to put on over her clothes. Sleeping under the stars alone would be a lot different than it had been with her father. Not that she was afraid to do it, but she wasn't exactly at ease, either. She hurried down the trail, trying to convince herself that the backpack was lighter now.

When she reached the stream she'd crossed earlier, she looked for a likely clump of bushes free of thorns and cactus spines in sight of the parking lot on the other side. Too bad she hadn't brought a plastic sheet. She could have set it up like a tent. Not that it would have been any warmer than sleeping on the bare ground, but it would have felt more sheltered. She hoped there weren't any bears around and that the snakes and scorpions were all asleep under their rocks. Probably she had nothing to fear. Probably. Oh, there might be a skunk that would find her, or at worst a javelina. Did packs of those big pig-like creatures hunt at night? She imagined the headline. "Young Girl Found Savaged by Javelinas at State Park."

A sudden screech made her shudder. What was killing what in the dark?

The sky had turned ink blue by the time she found a space behind a droopy-branched shrub. It was close enough to the stream so that the burbling water performed a lullaby that might shut out fearsome animal sounds. Pushing aside a few rocks, Tess dropped her backpack and curled up beside it. Not comfortable. She took some more clothes out to use as a pillow. Still not comfortable. She unloaded everything to find something she could use for a blanket, but nothing was big enough. Dad and she had had sleeping bags and a nylon tent when they'd camped here. Besides, it had been closer to summer. As she drank from the container of water she'd re-filled at the campground, Tess blinked back at the stars. Or were those planets that were winking at her? At least the moon was fat and full enough to act like a night-light.

Mom would think she was nuts to try sleeping here. But Dad would approve. He had a thing about getting close to nature. Blair claimed she liked camping, although not with very little kids and babies. "In a couple of years," she'd said, as if Tess would want to go with that whole crew. Of course, Blair would never offer to let Dad and Tess go off alone, the way Mom always had. Blair was a "family togetherness" fanatic.

They'd probably found the note by now, but they'd never find Tess here tonight, even if they were looking. Dad would call Mom to ask if she had arrived there yet. If

Tess were lucky, he'd just get the answering machine. It was hard to catch Mom in.

"Sleep," Tess told herself. She still had miles to go tomorrow. Idly she wondered where the cat was. Maybe it had found its owner in the campground after all. Or it could have set off for home. Cats could travel at night because they could see well in the dark. She hoped a coyote wouldn't get it, or an owl.

She closed her eyes, imagining herself homeless. The good thing about it would be no rules and regulations, no having to persuade anybody to let her do what she wanted. It might be hard physically, but she could get used to that. What would make it a lot better was having a companion, someone like her friend Ria maybe. Even the cat would be better than nobody.

Anyway, she wasn't homeless. Tomorrow she'd get to her mother's condo. She had food and money and she was doing fine, Tess assured herself. She closed her eyes and dozed, wishing the cat hadn't left her.

Something sharp digging into her side woke Tess. She rolled away from the sharp thing, and the warm pillow on her stomach dropped off. "Yow!" she yelled in terror.

In the moonlight she saw the cat, back arched in equal fear. It had leaped three feet away from her, out into the open. "Hey," Tess said, calming immediately when she realized who her pillow had been. "How come you came back to me? Come on, it's okay. I'm not going to hurt you." She waited.

The cat composed itself. It sat down facing her and kneaded its paws against the ground. "Come on," Tess coaxed. "Let's cuddle up again and be cozy."

It took the cat a while to consider her reasoning. Finally, when she'd about given up, it sauntered back to her. Tess reached out and stroked its head with one finger. She could feel the rumble of the cat's purr in her own chest. It was a lot sweeter than the shrill of the night bird and the shivery whoosh of the wind in the small leaves of the cottonwood trees. Carefully, Tess urged the cat closer. When it finally settled against her, still purring, she smiled. It was comforting to have a companion in the night, even if it was only a cat that didn't belong to her.

Chapter 4

Sunshine and birdsong gave Tess her wake-up call. She sat up and looked around. Her pack was there, but no cat. Had she dreamed it? No, there was the cat, drinking by the stream. Drinking? No way! It was holding some little animal down with its paw and eating it—a rabbit, judging by the long ears. Maybe this cat was tougher than she'd thought. "Like me," Tess said aloud.

Tough enough to hike an additional ten or fifteen miles today? She ached. Not only her hip, which hurt from the rock she must have been lying on during the night, but her shoulder joints and arms and neck were sore. She groaned. She could almost hear her mother say, "Well, what did you expect?"

Mom's idea of a good time was endless phone conversations, or eating out, or shopping and a movie with friends. She liked luxuriating in the bathtub for hours. She liked her job, too. Mostly Mom liked whatever she could wear make-up and silk clothes for. Too bad there was no phone nearby that Tess could use to call and beg a ride before her mother left for work. It would be worth owning up to how miserable she was right now in the great outdoors to be driven the rest of the way to the condo.

Even though the morning air was still cold, she repacked the extra clothes she'd put on for warmth during the night. She knew she'd warm up fast once she started walking. Her breakfast was peanut butter, crackers, and water. As for the cat, it had provided its own breakfast.

"So I'm off," she told the cat, which was now grooming itself by the stream. "Have a good life. And thanks for being my stomach warmer."

She left without looking back. When she got to where she had to recross the stream, she decided to walk on the rocks the cat had used instead of wading through the icy water. Halfway across, she slipped on a wet rock and fell in with a huge splash.

The shock of the chilling, fast-moving water made her scream. She struggled frantically to her feet and slogged over to the sandy bank, where she stood soaked and shivering. Now, should she keep moving or strip off her wet clothes and change into dry? She checked and found that the clothes in her waterproof backpack were dry. As for her wet hiking boots, she could carry them with her other wet clothes in the plastic bag that she had used for her food.

Back across the stream the cat sat watching her. While Tess pulled off her wet boots, it picked its way carefully across the rocks and arrived at her side looking calm and dry. Tess detected a smug smile on its face and scowled at it.

"So what? So I'm clumsy and you're not. But I can talk and you can't." What other advantages did she have? In her grumpy mood, she couldn't think of any.

Nobody was in sight. Cars were not allowed to stay in this parking lot overnight, so the lot was empty. She stripped down to her underpants and then, with a last look around, took them off and hurried into dry clothes. That was better and she was certainly wide awake now. She used one of the portable toilets, lined up like so many abandoned closets at the edge of the lot, refilled her water jug, and said to the cat, "Okay, I'm off. You coming?"

Apparently the cat was. When Tess got to the highway, there it was, three feet behind her. "Do you know about cars?" she asked it dubiously. A speeding car would take out the cat in a second.

"If you want, I could carry you—for a while, anyway." She crouched and waited for the cat to approach her. It reached up its head to be stroked.

"Hey," Tess said. "Is that all you think humans are good for?" But she stroked willingly, and then she tried to pick up the cat. It struggled in a sudden panic, leaped down, and took itself beyond her reach.

"Look, stupid," she said, "I was just being nice, offering you a free ride."

The cat twitched its tail contemptuously, as if it had heard that line before. The tail swished more rapidly. The cat made eyes at something skittering through the weeds. In an instant, it crouched, pounced—and missed. Then it sat to lick its shoulder with elaborate unconcern.

"Listen, Cat, the highway's not safe for you. You better let me carry you for your own good."

Tess swallowed hard. She was sounding just like her father. He was always draping chains around her for her own good. No leaving the house after school unless she checked in with an adult first and said where she was going. No reading past eleven at night, even if she was on the last chapter of a good book—because she needed her sleep. No talking back to teachers, even when they were clearly in the wrong. No doing chores when it suited her instead of her stepmother. No disobeying Blair, either. No chewing with her mouth open. Chained by stupid nos! Yet he'd looked hurt whenever she'd hinted that she'd rather live with her mother full-time and just see him on vacations and holidays.

Tess shrugged. "Okay. You do what you like, Cat. And if you get hit by a car, it's your tough luck."

When her parents had driven her along this highway between their homes, she hadn't realized how much of a climb it was. She seemed to be walking uphill forever. Besides, her backpack kept gaining weight on her. After what seemed like three miles up with no down in sight, she halted. A truck zoomed by shaking the airwaves and blowing dust and gravel at her legs, and no doubt at the cat's whole body.

Tess reached out to draw the cat in, but again it backed away from her.

"Just think about this," she said. "If I was going to hurt you, wouldn't I have tried something already?"

She sat down to rest, and as soon as her mind was off the cat, it appeared beside her. She looked down at it and sighed. "So it has to be your way, huh?"

The cat put its paws on her leg and jumped lightly into her lap. It settled itself into a cushiony ball. Tess stroked its head gently with one finger. What would it be like to have this animal as a pet? She smiled, imagining it. Ria would be so jealous. Cats were Ria's favorite, and like Tess, she'd never been allowed to have a real pet. They'd even had a bet about who could talk her folks into a pet first, and Ria had claimed to be the winner when she got a goldfish. "A goldfish doesn't count," Tess had insisted. "You can't pet it. And a pet has to be an animal you can *pet*. Get it?"

If all went well, she should be seeing Ria this afternoon. Maybe she'd surprise Ria when she got off the school bus.

Finally Tess stood and let the cat slip from her knees. "Off we go," she told it and started walking. Four trucks and then five cars whizzed by her. Where was the cat? It had suddenly disappeared.

Tess was so tired that she reconsidered sticking out her

thumb to hitchhike. But Dad would be livid if she got into trouble hitchhiking. "How could you be that foolish?" he'd ask, meaning, How could you be that stupid?

The mountains had finally changed shape alongside her right shoulder and become slumped, as if they'd melted. The desert here near the highway grew nothing but creosote bushes and cacti. Occasionally a housing development spread out to the foot of the mountains. On her left was an adobe wall with an entrance to some retirement village. Tess sat down again in the shade of the wall to drink. She'd finished half her jug of water when the cat appeared, a little dusty but still with her, apparently.

"Hi," Tess said. "You don't give up easy, do you? Me, neither. So I guess we've got something in common. Want some water?" She poured a capful and set it out. The cat lapped it up without hesitation, then turned away and began grooming itself with its tongue. Next it proceeded to climb into Tess's lap again, totally confident of its welcome. It stretched across her legs and rested its chin trustingly on her thigh.

"Tired?" she asked it. "Okay. I'll give you one more chance to be carried." She stood up, cradling the cat. It lay still in her arms. She tucked it into the crook of her right arm and switched the plastic bag full of wet clothes and boots to her left hand.

Before long the cat's weight began to increase. Tess's arm was sweating from the heat of its body. She wanted to put it down, but it seemed so content that she couldn't bring herself to disturb it. Yawning, she sat down in the dappled shade of a palo verde tree for another rest. Tess dozed. The cat dozed with her.

When she woke up, a woman was staring at her from the window of a car full of small kids. "What are you doing here in the middle of nowhere?" the woman asked.

"I'm traveling."

"Oh? To where?"

Tess frowned and didn't answer. She didn't want to smart-mouth the woman, because she sensed that here might be safe transportation. But what if the woman called the police about her? By now Dad had probably realized she wasn't at Mom's and had notified them. A daughter who wasn't accounted for at night would make him frantic. It was asking to get caught to keep going up a major road like Oracle, but that was the only way Tess knew to get to her mother's. Thinking fast, she concocted a story.

"My sister was supposed to drop me off at home, but we had a fight and she dumped me here. I don't live too far up the road, just a couple of miles."

"Get in," the woman said. "I'll take you home. It's dangerous to be wandering around the highway alone and in this heat."

"Can I bring my cat?" Tess thought to ask.

"Sure. We have one at home."

The woman introduced her to her three small children. A toddler was asleep in her car seat. An infant the same size as baby Sara was also asleep, and the third was a little boy who asked to pet the cat. He talked a mile a minute and told Tess all about how his cat had lost part of its tail to a coyote.

"You really shouldn't let your cat go outside," the woman said. "Those coyotes will eat any small cat or dog they can catch."

"I know," Tess said, noting the "shouldn't." It seemed to be most adults' favorite word next to "don't." At the intersection of the side road leading to her mother's neighborhood, Tess asked to be let off.

"No. I'll take you right to the door," the woman said.

"Please don't. I'll get yelled at for accepting a ride from a stranger," Tess said.

The woman frowned. "Yes, well, you shouldn't, of course."

Tess gritted her teeth, but she answered politely, "I know, but you looked so nice, and I was so tired, and besides, I figured it was safe with your kids being in the car, too."

The toddler who'd been sleeping picked that moment to wake up and start screaming. "Oh, no!" the woman said. "Now I'm in for it." She rummaged in a diaper bag for a bottle and handed it to the crying child, who batted it away and howled louder. That woke up the baby, who howled, too.

Tess opened the door beside her and stepped out with the cat, who had stayed on her lap the whole way. "I'll just get my backpack out of your trunk if you'll open it," she said.

"Okay," the woman yelled over her screaming children. "I guess you'll be all right." She picked up the milk bottle and put it in the baby's mouth. With her other hand, she popped open the trunk from a lever under the dashboard.

"Have a good day," Tess said cheerfully. She retrieved her belongings and headed away from the car, as if she were going down a street into a nearby section of homes. The cat padded after her. Tess waved and the little boy waved back. The mother was still trying to deal with her toddler's tantrum.

For half an hour, Tess hid with the cat behind a huge fountain that was under construction in someone's front yard. Then she set out again for the side road. From there it was only a mile or so to her mother's condo.

Chapter 5

Tess's old neighborhood was an isolated development surrounded by desert. Its three intersecting streets were packed with small tan houses, each with its own miniscule patio in back and courtyard in front. At the end of the main street were condos. These were smaller and shared common walls, but every unit had a plant-filled entranceway and a back patio. Behind them was a wash full of javelina and coyote tracks, where the birds chittered away the day in the mesquite and palo verde trees. Because it was midafternoon, the streets were deserted. People were either at work or in school. Besides, it was too hot for anyone to be outside.

"I've got to warn you, Cat," Tess said. "Mom won't have anything in the fridge for us. She's big on eating out. But there'll be ice cubes and cold water. Okay?" The cat was resting lightly against her chest with its head nestled under her chin. Its warm weight was uncomfortable on her arm, but Tess was still too touched by its show of trust to make it walk.

She wondered if her father had reached her mother last night. If not, when Mom got home from work, she'd be surprised to find Tess there on a weekday. As for the cat, that would be a bigger surprise. Mom might throw a fit and chase them both out the door, or she might laugh and let the cat stay. Unlike Dad, she wasn't predictable.

Tess had the key to her mother's condo on a string around her neck for safekeeping. Now she pulled it out. Instantly the cat jumped off her arm, as if the key were a weapon that Tess might use against it. It stopped on the walk, some five feet away and sat there, looking offended. But Tess suspected it wasn't likely to stroll off and leave her at this point.

"Maybe I can round up a can of tuna for you," Tess said. "There used to be one stuck in the back of the cupboard."

She turned the key in the lock—or tried to. It wouldn't turn. She pulled it out, reversed it and tried it that way. No luck. Had Mom moved without telling her? Tess bit her lip anxiously. The exhaustion she'd been ignoring suddenly crashed over her in a giant wave. She'd counted on getting into Mom's air-conditioned condo, where everything was cushioned and cheerful. Once more Tess tried the key. She even checked the number above the door. The condos *did* all look alike, but this one was definitely Mom's. There was the clay chicken pot Tess had given her for Mother's Day last year in the corner of the entrance patio. Frantically, Tess banged on the door. . . . Silence.

She took a deep breath. "Okay. So we can't get in until Mom gets home. What say we go to Ria's place?" Ria lived a few houses down from the nearly identical fake adobe house that had been Tess's when her mother and father were still together.

The cat flicked its tail against the patio tiles impatiently.

"Right. That's what we'll do," Tess said. She remembered the garage-size guesthouse in Ria's backyard. The key to it had always been kept under a steppingstone next to the sliding glass door. The backpack could safely be left out of sight behind a flowering bougainvillea on Mom's back patio, along with the plastic bag with the wet boots. Unencumbered, Tess ambled back down the street to Ria's house. The cat followed.

Judging by where the sun hung in the western sky, Tess wasn't surprised to see the yellow school bus that she and Ria used to take five mornings and afternoons a week at the entrance to their development. The bus flung out its stop sign and two little kids bounced out. They ran home in opposite directions. Ria emerged next. Her hair had been cut since Tess had last seen her over Easter vacation week, but she was as wispy and pale and pretty as ever.

"Ria!" Tess called.

It made Tess feel good to see her friend's face light up at the sight of her. "Hey, Tess! How come you're here? Did you run away from your father?"

"You got it. Except I walked—all the way. I think it must have been a hundred miles. I'm moving in with my mom," Tess said. "That is, if she still lives here. For some reason my key doesn't open her door."

"Oh, yeah." Ria nodded. "My mother said your mom had a big fight with her boyfriend and the police came. My mom said your mom had better get her locks changed to keep that man out, and probably that's what she did."

"Your mother saw the fight?"

Ria shrugged. It embarrassed her that her mother was such a busybody. Ria's mother worked part-time as a temp, doing office work at odd hours, but mostly she watched what was going on in the neighborhood. She was the one who complained if someone put garbage out on the wrong day and left it there on the street. She'd write an anonymous letter to anyone who used more than his allotted parking space in the guest parking lot. But most of the time, Ria's mother was good-natured and Tess didn't mind her. Mom, on the other hand, couldn't stand her.

The one Tess *didn't* like was Ria's father. He had a temper that resonated through the neighborhood whenever he lost it, which was frequently. Ria made excuses for her father. It was her nature to get along with people. Tess considered her to be wimpy that way. On the other hand, Tess credited the endurance of their friendship to Ria's good nature.

"So could I use your guesthouse to grab some shuteye while I wait for my mother to get home, Ria? I'm so tired and thirsty I can't even think straight," Tess said.

"You really walked all the way from your father's house? Boy, you must be pooped." Ria thought for a minute. "Mom will ask you a million questions if we stop by to say hello. Why don't you sort of sneak into the guesthouse, and I won't tell her you've come until you wake up?"

"Sounds good." Tess smiled. Ria could deal with sticky situations because her parents gave her lots of practice. "Do you mind if I bring the cat with me?"

"What cat?" Ria asked.

"The cat from the state park I stayed in overnight. That's where it found me." Tess looked around her— front, back, and both sides—without spotting the cat. No wonder Ria hadn't commented on it. It must have disappeared as soon as she had gotten off the bus. "Well," Tess said, "I *did* have a cat. It slept on my stomach last night and stuck with me all the way here. It'll probably show up again soon." After all, it didn't know anyone else but her around here.

"You're crazy, you know, Tess?" Ria said, but then she reverted to her usual accepting self and asked no further questions. "Okay," she said. "I'll go say hi to my mother and tell her how my day went. You'd better crouch down going past the kitchen window so she doesn't see you. She doesn't go into the guesthouse now that my brother and his wife moved into their own place, so that won't be a problem. Later you can tell me what happened."

"Don't I always tell you everything? . . . Uh, Ria, if you get a chance, I'm sort of hungry," Tess said.

"Right. I'll come by after we eat dinner and bring you something. Mom's used to me going to the guesthouse when I practice my recorder so it won't bother anybody."

"You're not still learning that dumb thing?"

"It's something to do. Life is pretty dull around here without you."

Tess was glad to hear it. "Well, you'll be seeing lots of me. . . . Unless Mom won't let me stay."

"You'll talk her into it. If she gives you a hard time, you can always promise to behave yourself." Ria laughed at the notion of Tess behaving herself. Tess laughed with her.

Tess ducked below the big kitchen window and circled around the windowless, boxlike guesthouse to the patio end, where sliding glass doors allowed entry. The key was where it was supposed to be under the steppingstone inscribed with a man wearing a sombrero. She washed her hands and face at the sink in the half bathroom, drank four glasses of water from the purple plastic glass, and used the toilet. The queen-size bed, which occupied most of the space in the room, was made up with pink sheets and a purple flowered comforter. It looked so inviting that Tess took a running leap and landed on her back in the middle of it. It felt wonderful under her sore arms and shoulders. She closed her eyes and was about to drop off to sleep when she heard an insistent meowing.

Wearily Tess got up and slid open the door. The cat stalked in, tail swishing with irritation at the delay in its welcome.

"Hey, you," Tess said. "What's your name, anyway? If we're going to be long-term buddies, I should know your name."

The cat hopped up on the bed and settled itself into a neat coil.

"I don't know what *you're* tired about. You got carried most of the way today," Tess said. "Although you *are* kind of small. And I didn't give you that tuna I promised you." She'd have to share whatever food Ria brought her tonight.

"Okay," Tess said. "So I guess I'll give you a temporary name." She lay down again. Her head was throbbing. "Cat, Puss, Gray—I don't even know if you're a boy or a girl." She sighed. The cat had closed its eyes, unconcerned about its identity. Later, Tess decided. When she woke up, she'd think of a name for it.

Chapter 6

The succulent odor of cooked hamburger and onion woke Tess.

"Good thing you left the door unlocked. That key under the tile's the only one, you know," Ria said as she came in with a plate of food. She set it down on Tess's stomach. The hamburger was on a bun next to broiled tomatoes topped by melted cheese. Tess's mouth began to water.

"What did you do, give me your whole dinner?" she asked.

"No. This is seconds. You know my mother always cooks too much."

Tess knew that. She had won Ria's mother's approval by raving about her cooking whenever she ate at Ria's house. That had been often, more often than Ria had eaten at her house. Cooking to Tess's mother meant heating take-out in the microwave.

Tess looked around for the cat, but it had disappeared again. She cut the hamburger in half with the plastic fork Ria had thought to provide and ate everything else on the plate.

"So what's that? Your midnight snack?" Ria asked about the remaining hamburger.

"It's for my cat."

Ria gave her a doubtful look.

"No, I'm not crazy. It hid when it heard you coming. . . . I guess it's shy of strangers. I've got to think of a name for it. What do you say, Ria? Magic? Starlight?"

"Yeah. Those were the names I made up for the cats I never did get," Ria said. "What's it look like?"

"Gray striped, green eyes, white chest, white feet, small and cute."

"Cuddles?"

Tess made a face.

"Okay. Let's find it, and then we'll name it."

The only place to hide in the empty room was under the bed, and sure enough, back in the farthest corner were two green eyes. Tess tried to coax the cat out with a pinch of hamburger, but it wouldn't budge. She didn't mention that it had been friendly enough to the boy in the campground, because that would hurt Ria's feelings. As it was, Ria asked wistfully, "How come it likes you so much better than me?"

"Must be my great personality," Tess said.

"But I'm nicer."

"Only on the outside. Inside, I'm nice, too."

"Not as nice as me," Ria said. "You told me so yourself. Remember? You said I was so sweet it made you sick."

"I must have been mad at you."

"Well, but it's true. That's how I stay out of trouble. Not like you. You couldn't care less about getting in trouble."

Tess considered that. "But I'm basically *sort* of nice, Ria. Aren't I?"

"Well, you're different. And I like you."

"You'd better," Tess said. "You're my one and only best friend." She grinned at Ria, who flopped on the bed next to her.

"Remember when we changed into each other's clothes and went to school and tried acting like each other?" Ria said. "It was hard for me. I couldn't even *make* myself get into trouble until lunch. I wouldn't clear my tray off the table. That was the baddest I could be. But you didn't last through first period being me."

Tess laughed. "I can't remember what I did, but I got detention for it. Mrs. Slide always gave me detention. She hated me."

"I think you doodled on my project folder. She didn't want her project folders messed up."

"Yeah. She was big on recycling."

The cat appeared. It crouched to spring onto the bed,

then hesitated, as if it were deciding whether to risk it with Ria there.

Tess considered her traveling companion. "If this cat's a girl, I could call her Ms. It kind of fits, because it's a pretty independent cat."

"You mean you're going to keep it?"

"I think it means to keep me," Tess said.

The cat made the leap. It landed on the foot of the bed near the plate with the remaining hamburger, and with a quick glance at Ria it grabbed a bite of the meat.

"Why don't you pick it up and turn it over," Ria said. "I can tell you if it's a girl or a boy."

Tess waited until the cat had finished eating, then reached for it, but it skittered away and hid under the bed again. "It'll come out when it's ready," she said.

"So why don't you like living with your father?" Ria asked. She leaned on her elbow, prepared to listen.

Tess told her all about the destruction of the Egyptian burial chamber and her father's refusal to help resurrect it.

"Umm," said Ria. "And that's it?"

"No. That was just the final straw. They've been clobbering me with rules and regulations ever since I got there. Like I should pick up my clothes and do my own wash and leave the door to my room open all day and keep it clean and put everything away. I'm supposed to eat when they do, chew with my mouth closed, compliment the cook, and help with the dishes. Also, they don't want me leaving the house unless I say where I'm going and to call if I'm late.

Last week Dad said I could make life pleasanter by smiling more. Can you believe it? And I don't do please and thank you enough to satisfy Blair. She says I set a rotten example for her kids. You'd think I was some badly trained two-year-old, the way they treat me."

Ria raised an eyebrow and asked, "But they're not yelling at you or hitting you or locking you in your room for a week, are they?"

"You've got to be kidding!"

"Well, this may be news to you, Tess," Ria said, "but kids our age are supposed to do that stuff you said. It's normal behavior."

"Come on, Ria! My mom never hassles me that way. She doesn't check up on where I'm going every minute of my life. *And* she doesn't act as if it's a criminal offense to bring home anything less than a B from school, either."

"Okay, fine," Ria said. "I hope your mother lets you stay with her. But I checked her condo and her car's not in the carport yet. My mom says she thought she saw your father's car there last night, but your mother wasn't around and he didn't stay long. Shouldn't you call him?"

"You mean, so he stops worrying?"

"Well, I bet he's already called the police."

"Yeah." Tess thought about it. "But if I call him, he'll want to know where I am, and if I tell him, he'll come haul me out of here before I even get to talk Mom into keeping me. I need to wait until Mom gets home tonight."

"Suppose she doesn't?"

"Why wouldn't she? Oh. You mean if she's on a business trip or something? Boy, I hope she's not." Tess chewed her lip. It was so hard to think of everything. She didn't want her father getting too frantic. What if he had a heart attack? He was such a worrier and he did have high blood pressure. It really was rotten of her to leave him in limbo. "What time is it?"

Ria checked her watch and told her it was six forty-five.

"If Mom's not home by eight, I'll call my father, okay?"

Ria shrugged. "He's your father."

"You like him, don't you?" Tess asked.

"Well, he's nice to me. Maybe he's a little picky, but he's not bad compared to some fathers."

Tess remembered how Ria's father yelled so loud about the dent her mother got in their car that the whole neighborhood heard him. He yelled about little things, too, like when Ria hadn't wanted to wear a new top her mother had bought her. Her own father might be rule-happy, but at least he didn't yell.

"Maybe I'll go camp out on Mom's doorstep until she gets home," Tess said. "Mind if I leave the cat here meanwhile?"

"What if it has to go potty?"

"Hmm. Yeah, okay. I'll take it with me."

"I could find a box and dig up some sand," Ria said eagerly. "There's a sandy spot by the fence that's soft enough to scrape up."

"You're glad about the cat, aren't you?"

"Yeah," Ria said. "I guess it'll get used to me if you stay."

"Well, if I don't, you get to keep it, because dear old dad is allergic to cats."

Ria smiled. "I'll work on getting it to like me—just in case." She went off to concoct a kitty litter pan. Meanwhile, Tess stuck her head under the bed and warned the cat not to mess in the room while she was gone. Then she slipped out of the guesthouse, leaving the door unlocked. Just in time she remembered to duck down below the kitchen window. Luckily the sliding glass doors of the guesthouse couldn't be seen from the main house so that if she had to come back and spend the night, Ria's folks wouldn't know that their guesthouse was occupied.

Half an hour later Tess's mother pulled into the carport, but she had a male passenger with her. He was wearing a white T-shirt that showed off his bulging arm and chest muscles, and he was laughing as he got out of the car. Tess ducked out of sight.

"I guess you can come in for a cup of coffee," Mom told the guy. "But I have to get up early for work tomorrow."

"Hey, trust me. I'll go when you want me to," the guy said. He touched Mom's arm familiarly, but she moved away from him to unlock her front door.

Tess felt a little nauseated seeing her mother with a strange man. Every new man in Mom's life made Tess queasy. Her head could accept that her mother was now free to go out with men other than Dad, but her stomach couldn't seem to. Whatever, this was no time to barge in on her mother—not if Tess wanted to be allowed to stay. She slipped around back to the patio to retrieve her gear. Carrying it to Ria's guesthouse hurt her overused muscles.

Ria had left sand in a box in the half bathroom, but she wasn't there. Tess asked herself how she was going to call her father. She couldn't use the phone in Ria's house, and to hike a couple of miles to the phone at the gas station might be dangerous now that it was getting dark. Also, she was too tired to attempt it. Guiltily she thought that it was mean to let Dad continue to worry about her. What she could do was go back to Mom's condo in another couple of hours, when the guy would likely be gone.

Tess unpacked the long T-shirt she used for sleeping, gave herself as good a washing up as she could at the sink, and went to bed. The cat promptly appeared. It plopped itself onto her stomach and began purring.

"It's easy for you," Tess told it. "You just latch on to somebody who'll take care of you and let them do the worrying. Well, you may have latched on to the wrong person, Ms. or Mr. Cat, whichever you are." She settled herself under the covers and closed her eyes. Worries nipped at her, but she was too tired to let them bother her. Soon enough she'd straighten everything out, she told herself. Meanwhile, she'd nap some more.

Chapter 7

It was morning when Tess woke up. No sooner did she open her eyes than Ria appeared with a plastic jar of juice and a bagel spread with cream cheese.

"How did you know I was here?" Tess asked.

"Your Mom called last night after ten when we were all asleep. She asked my mother if you were at our house. My mom was mad to be waked up, so I guess she wasn't very nice, and she said she hadn't set eyes on you. But this morning she asked me if I'd seen you. So I said, yes, and you were on the way to your mother, which was no lie. But I figured you mustn't be there yet. What happened?"

"She was with a guy when I saw her, so— You know." Tess shrugged. "I was going to take a nap and go back after he left, but I didn't wake up. I'd better catch her before she leaves for work. What time is it?" Tess dumped the cat off her stomach and swung out of bed.

"Seven fifteen. I see the cat used the pan." Ria nodded approvingly. "Did you put water out for it?"

"Oh, no. I didn't think of that."

"They need water," Ria said.

"Okay, I'll take care of it. See you after school, Ria, and thanks for the breakfast."

"That's okay," Ria said. "But you'd better get some cat food. Do you have any money?"

"Yeah, I'll get some food. Don't worry."

Ria hesitated in the doorway looking longingly at the cat, which was sitting on the floor watching both girls, first one and then the other.

Tess bent and picked the cat up. She turned it over, an indignity it submitted to tensely. "So is it a girl or a boy?"

"A boy," Ria said after a quick examination.

"Mr. then, or maybe Hombre? That's Spanish for man," Tess said.

Ria shrugged, "I don't know. It's your cat. I've got to go." She turned and ran for her bus.

The cat's eyes were dark and fearful and it was braced to escape. As soon as Tess released it, it fled back under the bed, as if Tess had betrayed it by confining it against its will. She knew the feeling. That's how it was for her living with Blair and Dad.

"See you later," Tess told the cat and went running off

to her mother's condo, barefoot and wearing only her long T-shirt and underpants.

Mom already had one leg in her car. She pulled it back out when she saw her daughter. "Tess! Where have you been?" Mom asked. "Your father's frantic. He left a million messages on my answering machine the night before last, but I wasn't home. And last night, he called me and kept insisting you must be with me. I got so mad that he wouldn't believe you weren't that I hung up on him." She stopped long enough to throw her arms around Tess and give her a hug that squeezed Tess so hard she pulled away first.

"I'll call and tell him it wasn't your fault," Tess said. "I'm sorry I scared you, Mom."

"Oh, I wasn't that scared. I figured you knew how to take care of yourself. You were with Ria, weren't you? But her rotten mother wouldn't admit it. That woman is so—"

"Ria's mother didn't know. And anyway, I was just there last night. I was hiding out in their guesthouse. It's a long story. I'll tell you later, but meanwhile, Mom—can I move in here with you? Please?"

Her mother's eyebrows went up and up and up at the question. "What happened?" She asked. "You and your father have the battle of the century or something?"

"I just can't be the way he wants. Or the way *she* wants, either," Tess said. "It's not my style."

Her mother twirled one of Tess's springy curls around her finger fondly, and said with a smile, "Mine, either.

Well, we'll talk about it tonight. I'll try to get home early. I need the sleep, anyway. Actually, I have to admit I drove all the way to Blair's house and back here looking for you like an idiot in the middle of the night in case . . . I know you can take care of yourself, but your father was so freaked out that he made me anxious."

"I'm sorry, Mom," Tess said. She had known her father would worry, but that she could upset her mother as well impressed her. "I'm really sorry. I won't do anything to make you mad at me again. I promise."

"Well, we'll see," Mom said. "It'll be fun to have you here—for a few days, anyway. I miss having you around to talk to when I need a sympathetic ear. But you know my lifestyle, Tess. I'm not home a whole lot. Which reminds me—the refrigerator's empty except for olives and salsa. Do you have any money?"

"Some," Tess said.

"Fine. Buy yourself lunch at the convenience store." Mom handed Tess a five-dollar bill. Then she looked down at Tess's bare feet and thought to ask, "You have anything to wear besides that T-shirt?"

"Yeah. I left some clothes in a backpack at Ria's."

Mom nodded. "It's nice that you and she are such close friends. Like sisters. I had a girlfriend like that once when I was a kid."

"Leah."

"Yeah. I told you about Leah?" Mom said wistfully.

"Leah and Clare, we were always together like a matched set."

"Uh-huh. She got mad at you for stealing her boyfriend and you lost her."

"He was such a jerk, too. I would have been a lot better off being faithful to Leah."

"Mom, that was twenty years ago."

"Yeah, I know." Her mother hugged her again, more gently this time, and Tess hugged her back. "Okay. I've gotta get to work or I'll be late, and you'd better call your father pronto. He sounded wild. And naturally he's blaming me for everything."

"I'll take care of it," Tess said.

"You do that. See you later." She slid into her low-slung fiery red car, blew Tess a kiss, and started the engine.

She had pulled out of the carport and was gone before Tess remembered that she couldn't get in the condo with the key she had. "Rats!" She'd have to go back to the guesthouse and stay there until her mother got home. Well, she had the cat to keep her company. But where was she going to call her father from?

As she walked back to Ria's guesthouse in her bare feet, trying to avoid the sharp gravel bits on the road, it occurred to Tess that she hadn't mentioned the cat to her mother. Mom claimed to hate cats. On the other hand, she was always game for new experiences. Once she'd met this cat, she had to see how special he was and like him. Because

Mom was a good sport and pretty fair about most things—
not about Dad, but most things.

"Isn't it amazing the way he follows me around just like
a dog?" Tess would point out. Although Mom had never
been much of a dog lover, either. There had to be a better
argument.

"You always said I'd get a pet some day. And this one is
no trouble. He can take care of himself if he has to." Not
bad. Then if Mom needed further persuasion, Tess could
promise that the cat wouldn't cost her anything because
Tess could pay for his food and kitty litter.

Dad gave her a generous allowance, so she could do that
easily. He'd never expected Tess to spend her allowance on
basic stuff the way Mom did. Mom claimed being poor as a
child had left her anxious about not having enough. Of
course, between the times when she hung on to stale bread
and a million plastic bags, Mom would splurge on clothes
and massages and quick trips to exotic places. Not that she
was extravagant only for herself. Last Christmas she'd
bought Tess a sound system to use at Dad's house. And
when Dad said horseback riding lessons for Tess were too
expensive, Mom had offered to pay for them. Of course, it
had turned out no one was available to drive Tess to the
riding stable at the right times, but Mom had meant well.

Competition over doing things for her seemed to be
how her parents related to each other since their divorce.
Sometimes they got so intense that it made Tess wonder if
they were acting out of love for her or just getting back at

each other for the bad parts of their marriage. After all, she knew she wasn't the most lovable kid in the world—not sweet like Ria or Annie, not good-looking like Brian. She was the child who caused her parents to get angry phone calls from teachers. Mostly they complained that they couldn't get her to work, but sometimes they called because she'd disrupted their classes by doing things like propping her feet on her desk or arguing with them.

The school calls embarrassed Dad and irritated Mom. After one of them, Tess had heard her father say, "I guess we haven't done a very good job of raising her."

"*We* haven't, or do you mean *I* haven't?" Mom had asked. And they'd gone tearing into each other. No doubt about it. Her parents had reason not to be too crazy about her.

As for loving them—well, she expected she did. They weren't perfect, but they were the only parents she had. Besides, there'd been good times with both of them. Like the camping trip with Dad when the male deer had barred their way up the canyon until the female he was guarding crossed the trail. And like Mom's hilarious attempt to bake cookies for Tess's fourth-grade party. Mom had let the first batch burn and forgotten to put sugar in the second batch. On the way to the market to buy packaged cookies, Mom had burst out crying and called herself a failure as a mother. Tess had had to say a lot of gushy stuff to comfort her then, but she hadn't felt as if she was lying.

Ria's mother's car was gone from their carport and so

was her father's truck, but just in case, Tess ducked under the kitchen window as she passed it. The day was too beautiful to spend in the dimly lit guesthouse, and there was still the problem of where to find a phone to call her father. She had to do that before he wore himself out worrying.

She could make the call from the convenience store, buy some stuff for lunch, and get food for the cat. Then she could hang out on Mom's patio or else in the guesthouse until Ria got home from school. Catching Mom when she got home from work might be harder because her hours were so erratic. But she'd promised to be early tonight and she might be, especially if she remembered Tess didn't have a key for the new locks.

"So you want to go on another long walk with me, Mr. Cat?" Tess asked. The cat was still flopped out like a rag doll on the unmade bed. Tess got clean clothes out of her pack and dressed herself. When she held the front door open, the cat lifted its head and yawned at her.

"Come on," Tess said. "You don't want to sleep all day, do you?"

Apparently not, because he leaped lightly off the bed and strolled out the door ahead of her. She set off without checking to see whether he was following or not. If he chose to hang out in Ria's yard, that was his business.

"I could call you Smoky because you're gray," Tess mused when she reached the entrance to the development and found that the cat was indeed with her—not exactly at her heels, but close behind. "Or Mouse. But I hate that name. It's stupid to call somebody something they're not. How about Buddy? You make a good buddy the way you follow me everywhere."

The cat regarded her without venturing an opinion, and Tess stopped worrying about it.

Sunlight glinted off every shiny pebble on the road. Once the cat disappeared into some spear-headed grass to chase a small, dark shadow. Heat pressed against Tess's shoulders. Cup-shaped yellow flowers bloomed on masses of prickly pear, but the brittle bush that had made such a bright yellow frieze along the road for a while was browning. By afternoon the temperature would be in the nineties. This morning it was still cool enough, though. It was nice not to be in school, trying to stay awake while a teacher droned on about something that had absolutely nothing to do with any life Tess wanted to live.

The only class she really enjoyed was art. She'd won an award for her weird sculpture last year, and her watercolor of the mountains had been hung in the cafeteria as a "student best." Being an artist would be an okay job. . . . Maybe.

The phone was on a pole outside the convenience store near the gas pumps. The cat sat down in the shade next to the building while Tess put in her quarter and tapped out her father's number.

Her stepmother answered. "Oh, Tess! Thank God. We were frantic," she said in her high, silky voice. "Where are you?"

"I'm okay. Where's Dad?"

"He had to go to work. The police said since I was going to be home today that he might just as well—"

"Uh-huh, okay," Tess interrupted. "Just tell Dad I'm fine. He doesn't have to worry. I'm going to stay with my mother."

"You're with your mother? But she said—"

Evading the question, Tess continued, "She says I can stay with her. Soon as she has time, I'll get her to drive by so I can collect the rest of my stuff. Okay?"

"Tess, it's not okay. Your father will want to know—"

"I've got to go now," Tess said. "Bye." And she hung up.

"There," she told the cat. "That takes care of that. They don't need to know every little thing. They'd just want to mess with the details so they can make it come out their way."

Chapter 8

Tess stepped into the convenience store and bought herself a cold fruit drink. While she sipped it, she shopped for a bag of cat food and some bread and cheese for herself. Milk, she decided—that would be good for both of them. And four candy bars in case she needed cheering up. Also, she could share one with Ria later. Ria's mother wouldn't let her buy candy because it rotted her teeth. Ria was always getting cavities. Tess, on the other hand, never had anything wrong with her teeth, or any other part of her. Except for the time she'd broken an arm climbing up a steep roof to rescue a kite.

The cat seemed mopey on the way back, so Tess picked him up and carried him. He made a counterweight for the bag of groceries on her other arm. Already he seemed used to her carrying him, and he relaxed, resting his head lightly against her. "Are you my guy?" she asked him fondly, "are you my loverly guy?"

The next four hours dragged by so slowly that Tess decided it was more boring to be waiting for Ria than to be in school. She put aside the sketchpad on which she'd been drawing the plants in Ria's backyard. What else was there to draw? The empty guestroom didn't look promising. The walls were painted pink over bare cinder block, and only one wall boasted a picture. Not much of a picture— just some pink flowers climbing up an adobe wall. She should have brought watercolor crayons with her. Then she could have painted a picture of Ria's backyard as a gift in return for putting up with her. The pencil sketches she'd done were okay, but not worth hanging.

There *were* art supplies that Tess had left behind in Mom's hall closet for weekend use. And Mom had said she'd get home early. Of course, she didn't always keep her word. She meant to, but she'd get distracted by something and forget.

"Meow?" the cat asked.

"Sure," Tess told him. "Whatever you say."

He looked at her and kneaded the coverlet with his front paws. Tess stroked his head with one finger. He closed his eyes blissfully and pushed against her finger, tilting his head so that she could reach his white throat.

Tess wondered how important the guy with the muscles was in her mother's life. Not too important yet, if he had

only been invited in for coffee last night. And what if Mom
had to do a lot of traveling—say, during the summer when
school was out? Well, then Tess could hike to the convenience store for food and hang out with Ria most of the
time. She'd manage.

"Cat," Tess said to her companion, "we don't need anybody, do we?"

The cat blinked at her wide-eyed.

When it seemed about time for Ria to be coming home,
Tess walked to the school bus stop with the cat behind her.
Ria got off with a boy. Gunther Wool. Tess remembered
him from last year when they'd both been in sixth grade.
He'd been short then. Now he was tall.

"Hi, Gunther," Tess said. "What are you doing here?"

"He came to look for horny toads in that desert wash
behind our development," Ria said. "I forgot to tell you
about it. You can come with us if you want."

"Horny toads? In the wash?" Ria never liked going into
that dry streambed where the water ran down from the
mountains during the monsoon season, because she was
afraid a rattlesnake would get her there.

"That's the most likely place to find them," Gunther
said. He was an A student, a biology nut. Tess wondered
when his interests had expanded to include Ria. It struck
Tess that she'd been away longer than she'd thought.

Ria's mother was still at work. In Ria's kitchen, the three
of them snacked on home-baked molasses cookies and
soda before starting off on the hunt.

"Gunther is my boyfriend now," Ria told Tess quietly as she poured more soda into Gunther's glass.

Last year it had been Alan, who was a good dancer and not much else. Ria usually had a boyfriend in her life. Being pretty and sweet, she attracted boys like bees. Sometimes Tess had enjoyed the boyfriend's company and sometimes—like when Alan had been in Ria's life and Tess had nicknamed him the "duh" boy—she had not.

"So Gunther, you must have grown a foot since I last saw you," Tess said.

"Just six inches. I'm in a growth spurt."

"Are you a basketball star yet?" Tess said, meaning it sarcastically.

"Well, all of a sudden they want me on the team." He smiled as if that pleased him.

Tess imagined it would since he hadn't had many friends before. "And you're still into bugs and roaches and things?"

"Horned lizards. Around here they're mostly called horny toads and they're really interesting."

"I'll bet," Tess said.

"No, really. Did you know . . ." He launched into something about how a horny toad could squirt blood from its eye and hibernate, but she didn't bother listening. She hated lectures. Anything that sounded even vaguely like a lecture caused her brain to click off automatically. All she could hope was that Gunther wasn't going to be around every afternoon.

"Where's the cat?" Ria asked.

"The cat?" Tess leaped up and ran outside. She remembered him following her to the bus stop, but after that—She found the cat sitting in front of the door to the guesthouse in the shade.

"I'm sorry. I forgot about you," Tess apologized. She let him in and he went immediately to the toilet and crouched on the seat to drink from the bowl.

"Oops. I forgot to give you water, didn't I?" Tess ran back to the main house and borrowed a bowl from Ria. When she returned to the guesthouse, the cat was asleep on the bed. She filled the bowl for him and left him there, figuring he had everything he needed for the moment. Obviously, he didn't take to strangers.

Gunther's search through the thick growth of cacti and ominous-looking weeds and rocks went on for a long hot while. Finally, after Tess had sideswiped a cholla and gotten a mess of thorns in her leg, she told them she'd see them back at the ranch and returned to the guesthouse alone.

The only good thing about Ria's boyfriends, Tess thought as she plucked out thorns, was that Ria didn't take them too seriously. She had always been willing to put a boy off to another time if Tess wanted to do something with her—like searching for gemstones or making funny signs or costumes or sleeping over at each other's house. On the other hand, Ria liked being courted. She got excited when a boy called her. She'd be thrilled by some soppy

Valentine card. Thinking about it, Tess realized special attention would make her feel good, too—if she ever got any.

"Like you chose me," she told the cat. He lifted green-almond eyes to her face and listened to her with his ears perked up and moist button nose tilted her way.

"You're cute, you know?" she told the cat.

Probably he knew. He began grooming his white paws.

Ria knocked on her door and stuck her head into the guesthouse. "Your mother's car is there," she said.

"Is Gunther gone?"

"Yeah, he went home. His mother picks him up on her way back from her aerobics class twice a week. That's when we usually see each other, after school."

"Did you find any horny toads?"

"Just Gunther," Ria joked.

Tess laughed. "Is he a toad?"

"Well, he keeps trying to kiss me."

"And do you let him?"

"Sometimes," Ria said. "I like kissing."

Tess had no response to make to that. She'd never been kissed except by her parents—and Annie.

"Are you going home to your mother, then?" Ria asked, "or do you want to come into the house and say hi to my mom and have dinner with us? Now you can say you're here because you're visiting your mother. You don't have to hide out anymore."

"Right, but I guess I'll go home. I need to talk to Mom."

"Then call me later and tell me what she says."

"Yeah."

Tess had already packed and made up the bed so that the room looked as it had when she'd first come in. She carried the cat's litter box and bowls for food and water and hefted the pack on her back again. When she stepped outside the guesthouse, the cat followed her promptly. Ria bent down and the cat allowed himself to be petted.

"Good, he's getting used to me. So what's his name?" Ria asked.

"I don't know. Buddy maybe?"

"Buddy? That sounds like a dog's name," Ria said scornfully.

"Umm. Well, why don't you think of something."

"It's your cat."

"Think anyway, and thanks for hiding me. I'll see you later."

"Sure," Ria said.

Tess sneaked by the kitchen window for what she expected was the last time. She hiked to her mother's condo and rang the bell.

"Honey!" Mom said. "I'm so sorry about the key. I forgot that the locks are changed. Where did you spend the day?"

"Gasping in the desert," Tess said. "Let me in. I'm dying of thirst."

"Your father just called. I explained about the key and that I suspected you were with Ria."

"You didn't? Now he's going to think you're irresponsible."

"He's probably right. If you weren't so independent, you'd never have survived a mother like me."

Tess smiled and walked past her, lugging her pack and followed by the cat.

"Yikes!" Mom shrieked like an alarm system gone haywire. "Get that thing out of my house. Shoo, shoo, shoo!" She made motions with her hands at the cat, who promptly skittered under the couch.

"Now, listen, Mom. This is my buddy," Tess said.

"You listen. I said *you* could live here." Mom was shaking as she spoke. "I didn't say anything about bringing in stray animals."

"He's like me, Mom. He takes care of himself."

"I hate cats," Mom said. "I hate, despise, and loathe cats." She looked so freaked out that Tess fetched the cat out from under the couch and held him protectively in her arms.

"Mom, this cat is pretty nearly a dog. He follows me everywhere. He's slept with me for three nights."

"Three nights? You could be full of fleas."

"He doesn't have fleas."

"How do you know?" Mom demanded.

"Because . . . How about we take him to the vet and get him checked over so you'll be sure he's healthy? I'll pay for it."

"No." Mom folded her arms.

"No, what? No, I don't have to pay for it, or no, you don't want to bother with a vet?"

"No cats in my house. Not ever."

"If you knew him, you'd love him, Mom. Really, this is a special cat."

"Take your pick, Tess, me or the cat."

It was like a knockout blow, and just when Tess had thought she was home free.

Chapter 9

Tess carried the cat outside to the patio and sat down on a lounge chair to think. The cat coiled itself into a comfortable oval on her lap and went to sleep.

"Hey," Tess said, nudging the limp animal with her knee, "this is your problem, too, you know. Wake up and help me figure out what to do."

The cat gave her an accusing green glance. He stretched one elegantly white-booted, gray-and-black-striped front leg, and then the other. Then he went back to sleep.

"I could let you live outside and give you food and water every day. But if a coyote doesn't get you, a fox or owl might." Not to mention that any tree a housecat might climb to escape a predator was full of thorns.

"Maybe we could build you a cage outside, a big one

with a shady area," Tess mused. But Mom's back patio was small, and she wasn't going to allow it to be caged in for the sake of a cat. Besides, a room-size cage would probably cost more than Tess could afford.

"Well, I'm not going back to Dad, not even for you," Tess told the cat. She stroked him, and his purr was as soothing as waves shushing the shore. "Besides, Dad's allergic to cats and my stepmother's a neatness freak. I bet she hates cats as much as Mom does.

"Think," Tess told herself. While she poked around her brain for an idea, she draped the cat carefully over her shoulder. His only reaction was to tuck his head against her neck, where his whiskers tickled her as she walked back to Ria's house.

Ria's mother opened the door. "Tess! How nice to see you. Ria told me you'd come to live with your mother full-time. I'm so glad, because Ria's been in a blue funk ever since you left. Come on in." She stepped aside to let Tess pass into the living room. "That's a cute cat," Ria's mother continued in her usual run-on monologue. "Is it yours?"

"Not exactly, but he's sort of adopted me." Tess was wary of confiding her problem to Ria's talkative, takeover mother. "Is Ria home?"

"She's in her room. I'm sure you know where that is. But when you come out to the kitchen, I made rice pudding. You always liked my rice pudding."

"Yum," Tess said. "Yes, I love it." She gave Ria's mother

a smile and sped down the hall, keeping a tight hold on the cat. He had tensed at being in a strange place and was digging his claws into her.

"Relax," she told him. "You're safe here."

She barged into Ria's bedroom and blurted out, "Ria, I need help. My mom hates cats and won't let me stay with her if I keep him."

"So leave him with me."

Tess stared blankly at her friend. "You think your mother would let you?"

Ria shrugged. "I could tell her he can stay in the guesthouse if she's worried about the furniture. She's always said I could have a cat someday."

"Then why don't you have one?"

Ria hesitated. Her face took on the secretive look she always got when there was something she didn't want to reveal about her family. "Well, my father's sort of funny about pets. Sometimes he's okay, but then he doesn't want to be bothered." Ria shrugged. She had never been willing to say anything bad about her parents. But once Tess had been there when Ria's father had come home angry. His yelling and cursing had been scary. Neither Tess's father nor her mother ever got that furious.

"What do you mean by 'sort of funny'?" Tess asked.

"Oh, you know. Like that dog we inherited?"

"You only had him for a week."

"Yeah. Dad blamed that dog for everything. He didn't like poor Patches."

"Yeah. I remember. He took him to the animal shelter." Ria had gotten hysterical about that, so Tess had called the shelter and been told they didn't have any dog named Patches. No terriers at all had been brought in that week. Tess hadn't given her friend the bad news. What she'd told Ria was that Patches had already been adopted. Tess had even made up a story about a couple with a little boy who was lame and really needed a dog.

Ria had believed her and been comforted. As to what really happened to Patches, only Ria's father knew. And when Tess had asked him, he'd mumbled something about finding a good family for the dog. Tess hadn't exactly believed him, but she'd figured she'd done as much as she could. Whatever had happened to Patches had already happened.

"Now what's that cat up to?" Tess said. He had squeezed out of her arms and was exploring Ria's doll collection. He sniffed and poked so delicately along the shelves of costumed dolls from all over the world that not one was disturbed. Tess had to smile as the cat reached a paw to the shelf below to play with the red silk ribbon on a doll's hat.

"Isn't he a character?" she said.

"Let me keep him," Ria said again. "Maybe Dad'll like him."

Reluctantly Tess agreed. "I guess he'd be better off here than running around loose. Okay. Let's see what your mother says."

They shut the cat inside Ria's bedroom and went to the kitchen. Ria's mother smiled at them and asked if they were ready for a treat.

While they spooned up her warm, creamy rice pudding, Ria's mother considered taking in the cat. "You say your mother won't let you keep it?"

"Mom hates cats," Tess said, "and my father's allergic to them."

"You could take it to the animal shelter," Ria's mother said.

Tess ignored that suggestion. No way was she about to put her cat any place where it might be destroyed. "This is a very special cat," she said. "He's kind of like a dog the way he follows you, and he's very smart."

"And he's clean and careful," Ria added. "He wouldn't be any bother, Mom. I'll take good care of him."

The eagerness in Ria's voice reminded Tess of how much her friend had longed for a pet. But did it have to be *her* cat? And yet if she couldn't keep him herself, the next best thing would be for Ria to have him. At least he'd be near enough for regular visits. It would be kind of like joint custody.

"All right. We'll see how your father feels about it," Ria's mother said. "But if he says no, Tess will have to find him another home. Understood?"

"Understood," both girls said in unison.

Leaving the cat in Ria's bedroom, Tess ran down the street to her mother's condo. Mom let her in and blew her a kiss, but she kept talking to someone on the phone, which she had tucked under her ear. ". . . so he's too young for me, so what? If he doesn't care, why should I?"

She had to be talking to Barbara. Barbara and Mom had worked together and become buddies after Mom's divorce, but then Barbara had quit her job and moved to Phoenix. Whenever Tess wasn't around to confide in, Barbara was the one Mom called.

"Be right back," Tess told her mother and she took off again to transfer the cat's litter box and food to Ria's house.

"Want to play a game?" Ria asked her, after she'd stowed away the cat's belongings.

"No, I need to ask my mother some stuff," Tess said. "You get cozy with the cat. And think of a name for him, huh?"

"Right," Ria said. "Thanks." She beamed, as if Tess had given her a wonderful gift.

Mom was still on the phone when Tess returned. That gave Tess time to stuff her underwear, T-shirts, and sweater into the drawers of the end table and lay her sketchbook on top of it next to the lamp. She made up her bed on the pull-out couch and put her toothbrush and comb and deodorant in the bathroom and her empty backpack in the utility closet. That was it. She was settled in. But the satisfaction she'd expected to feel didn't come. She wanted her cat back, his weight in her arms, the satiny feel of his fur under her fingertips. She missed him already.

When her mother finally got off the phone, Tess asked, "So how come you had to change the locks?"

"You remember Haig, that man from the IRS I was seeing? Well, he got rough and threatened me after I kicked him out. It's no problem, Tess. There's another new key in the kitchen drawer." Mom got up and headed for the tiny kitchen. "I'd better give it to you before I forget. Then I've got to get dressed."

"You're going out tonight?" Tess was dismayed.

"I've got a date with my personal trainer. He's a real sweetie."

"Is he the guy who came home with you last night?"

"How did you know about him?" Mom looked puzzled.

"I was watching, but when I saw you had company, I didn't bother you," Tess said.

"Oh, right," Mom said as if she approved of that. "Well, he lives near here. He's renting with another guy. What'd you do with the cat?"

"Gave it to Ria."

"Good. I suppose her mother made some remark about me not letting you keep it?"

"No. She didn't say anything."

"That woman is such a busybody. She asks the most personal questions whenever I bump into her. You'd think we were friends, which we're not. I stopped going shopping on the way home from work, because that's when she shops."

"Did you talk to Dad about my staying here?"

"He doesn't like it. He says you're going to be on your own too much. I told him you liked being on your own."

"Yeah," Tess said. She did, but she was disappointed that her mother wasn't staying home with her on the first night of their new life together. "You know that cat followed me all the way from Catalina State Park?" Tess said.

"Did he really? Which one do you like better?" Mom asked. She was holding up a short red sheath dress and a multicolored thing that looked like a sarong.

"Are those dresses new?"

"I just bought them. I wanted something young-looking for this guy. He's only twenty-eight. . . . I guess the red," she advised herself. She shed her skirt and blouse, dropped them on the nearest chair and slipped on the sheath. It followed her every curve and showed a lot of her legs.

"Mom," Tess said. "Where are you going with this guy?"

"To a bar near here. He says it's real funky."

"Don't wear that dress."

"Why? There's nothing to it. It's just a simple sheath."

"You said it. There's nothing to it."

"Hey, I know I'm your mother, but I'm only thirty-three. You may not think so, but that's still young."

Tess shook her head. "It's like you're showing off how sexy you are, and you don't even know what kind of people go to that bar."

"Listen," her mother said coldly, "I said you could stay here, but not if you're going to sound like a recording of your father. You do your thing. I do mine. Okay?"

Tess was chastened. Had she been sounding like Dad with his endless safety precautions? "Yeah, okay."

After sharing a microwaved pizza with her, Mom left. Tess switched on the TV, but she kept thinking about her mother being ogled by strange men in a funky bar. At ten o'clock, she called her father.

This time she was lucky. He was the one who answered.

"So Dad, I'm sorry for making you worry like that," Tess began.

"Tess! Where are you?"

"At Mom's . . . Why does she hate cats so much?"

"She's phobic about them. Always has been."

"And you're allergic to them?"

"Well, I had asthma as a child and cats were one of the things I was allergic to. Why?"

"I had this cat and I had to leave it with Ria, but I'd really like to keep it. He's a great cat."

"I know, I know. You're a deprived child because we never let you have a pet," Dad said impatiently. "Well, I'm sorry, but you've had a lot of other advantages."

"Like what?" Tess asked.

Her father sounded outraged as he answered heatedly, "Like being sheltered and cared for and sent to school and camp and swim lessons and all that."

"But I thought every kid has a right to those things," Tess said.

"They should have, but not every kid is well treated," Dad said.

"Okay. So you're a good parent," Tess said. "But you make me feel like I'm locked in a cage."

He sputtered. "How can you talk to me like that? You have no respect for your elders. It's no wonder you're always in trouble."

"Come on, Dad. I'm not 'always in trouble.' I've never even been suspended."

"No doubt that comes next."

"Well, if I'm so horrible, you should be glad I'm living with Mom now."

"I am *not* glad," he said. "It's a bad idea. Your mother's not there enough to supervise you."

"I don't need supervising."

"Don't you? You think you're a grownup at twelve?"

"I'm thirteen."

"Not for a month. Look, Tess, I want you back. You belong here with Blair and me."

"You've got plenty of kids there without me," Tess said. "It'll be easier with me gone. Anyway, Dad, it's not that I don't love you. I just hate living with you."

"Thanks," he said bitterly. "That's some reward for twelve years of trying to be a good father. You hate living with me."

Tess didn't say anything. He hadn't heard the first part of what she'd said, or he didn't believe it.

Finally he said, "So where is your mother?"

"Umm. She'll be back soon. . . . Dad, I don't want to leave the cat with Ria. He's my cat. He picked me out."

"Well," her father said, "what do you expect me to do about that?"

They waited through a silence.

"So how's Annie?" Tess asked finally.

"She keeps asking for you. Wants to know where her Tess is. I thought she was asking me for her dress and went to her closet and kept showing her dresses until she started to howl. Brian had to tell me she didn't want a dress—she wanted you."

"She'll get over it," Tess said.

"No doubt. And you'll get over your attachment to the cat. Right?"

Tess gulped and said, "You mean, what's gotta be is gotta be. That's what you always tell me."

"Not in English as bad as that. Listen, your mother and I have joint custody. That means you have to spend *some* time with me whether you like it or not. So I'll expect you here for weekends."

"Are you going to pick me up and deliver me?"

"I'll discuss it with your mother. When she gets home, ask her to call me."

"Not tonight, Dad. She's tired."

"Where did she go?"

"Just out to get some stuff," Tess said vaguely. Then she changed the subject. "So how's Blair doing? I'll bet she's glad to be rid of me."

"Blair likes you, Tess."

"No. She doesn't."

"She says you're gutsy."

"Yeah?"

"I told her you took after your mother."

"I don't."

"But you do in some ways."

"Yeah? According to Mom, I sound like a recording of you."

He snorted. "Sometimes I doubt you inherited anything from me."

"Well, I've got your smile and your eyes. Everybody says so."

"Look, Tess, just remember you're my daughter. I can't forget that and I hope you won't, either."

Some desperation in his tone touched her. Was he saying, in his own peculiar way, that he loved her? Or was he saying that he owned her? Before she could decide, he started talking about school and what she needed to do about it, so she stopped listening to him.

"Don't worry. I'm not planning to be a seventh-grade dropout. Good night, Dad," she said and hung up. When the phone rang again, meaning he hadn't finished telling her what she needed to do, she didn't answer. She heard his voice on the answering machine and put her fingers in her ears. One advantage of being at her mother's condo was that she didn't have to listen to her father's lectures.

Tess went to sleep on the couch wondering how the cat

was doing. Was it sleeping in Ria's bed? Lying on Ria's stomach? Purring in Ria's arms? I'm jealous, Tess told herself, and there isn't a thing I can do about it.

Monday she might as well go back to her old school here and pick up seventh grade where she'd left off at the school in Blair's and Dad's neighborhood. Even though it was what Dad wanted her to do, she'd do it. It would be better than spending her days hanging around an empty house alone.

Chapter 10

The click of the key in the front door lock woke Tess that night. She lifted her head above the back of the couch and watched her mother negotiate the crossing to her bedroom. Judging by her mother's stiff and careful posture, Tess guessed she'd been drinking but wasn't very drunk. She'd be okay in the morning. Good. Tess closed her eyes and went back to sleep.

The alarm rang in her mother's bedroom at six, but Tess heard no getting-up sounds. "Mom, are you awake?" she called. She rolled off the couch and stepped to the open bedroom door. Clothes were strewn over the floor where they'd been dropped. The lump under the bedcovers was Mom.

"It's Saturday. Do you have to work today?" Tess asked.

A tousled head appeared with heavy lidded eyes. A

hand reached out to turn off the alarm. "Oh, rats, why did I stay out so late? I've got to make a presentation this morning."

"Want me to get you anything?"

"No, no. I've gotta take a shower. . . . Maybe some coffee." She stumbled off to the bathroom naked. Her mother's lack of modesty jolted Tess, even though she'd recently decided she was wrong to be so inhibited and her mother had the right attitude.

Tess had learned how to operate the coffeepot when she was six. That had been necessary because, although coffee was essential to her mother's mobility, she hated getting up and never remembered to set the pot on a timer the night before. Dad didn't drink coffee. He didn't like Mom's dependence on it, either, so he wouldn't prepare it for her even when they had lived together.

Tess fixed the coffee and found one stale bagel in the bread drawer. She cut it in half and stuck it in the toaster. Nothing was in the refrigerator to put on it. While Tess waited for her mother, she ate her half of the dry bagel at the counter where her mother usually sat to drink her coffee.

"You look pretty good, considering," Tess said when Mom came out dressed in a tailored suit and the latest style in shoes.

"Yeah . . . considering. Do the bags show under my eyes?"

"Just a little. Did you have a good time?"

"It was okay. He's really young. I mean, even the jokes." Mom shook her head. "But he's cute and he likes me." She shrugged. "So what'll you do with yourself today, sweetie?" She sipped her coffee and thanked Tess for making it. She even nibbled at the stale half bagel.

"Oh . . . I'll hang out with Ria as long as you're busy. You coming back later?"

"Actually, I promised Barbara I'd drive up to Phoenix tonight and spend tomorrow with her. I told her I might be bringing you along. You like her, don't you?"

Since Barbara had quit her job and moved away, Tess hadn't seen anything of her. She was a single woman who told long, involved stories about her misadventures with men. She'd never married but always had a man in her life, every one of whom had disappointed her in some way. Listening to her mother and Barbara talking about their boyfriends was as interesting as listening to a soap opera for Tess.

"Sure, I like Barbara," Tess said. "I'll bring my sketchpad and there's always TV."

"Okay, and what are you going to do about school next week?"

"I'll go Monday on the bus with Ria, just like I used to."

"Good. Because we don't want the truant officer coming after us," Mom said.

The trip to Phoenix went about as Tess had expected. On the way up Saturday night, Mom quizzed her about Blair and Dad and the new baby, but she lost interest when Tess didn't have anything negative to say.

"I'm glad your father found such a perfect wife," Mom said sourly when Tess had finished an honest accounting of life at Blair's house.

"She's not as pretty as you, or as fun," Tess said.

"Oh, she's attractive in her way," Mom admitted.

"I like your way better," Tess said.

"Do you, honey?" That earned Tess a one-armed hug. But then Mom put in a tape, and for the rest of the way they listened to pop tunes played too loud to allow for conversation.

Barbara screeched happily when she saw Tess. "You're getting better looking every year," Barbara said. "Do you have a boyfriend yet?"

"No, I have a cat."

"You let her have a cat?" Barbara asked Mom in amazement. "I thought you hated cats, like me."

"I do," Mom said. "I told her she couldn't keep it in the house, so she gave it to her friend."

"Oh." Barbara frowned at Tess and shuddered. "Cats give me the creeps."

"But why?" Tess asked. She turned to her mother. "Did you have a bad experience with one or something?"

"No, I just don't like the way they slink around and kill things."

"Lots of people hate cats," Barbara said. And that was the end of her interest in Tess. She sat Mom down on the couch and launched into the saga of her latest relationship. "I tell you, Clare, this guy had everything," Barbara began with enthusiasm. Her stories almost always ran from a high of expectation to a low of disapproval. This one was so interminable on its way down and out that Tess fell asleep on the floor in front of the TV in the middle of it. Barbara and Mom were still talking the next morning.

Tess tried sketching Barbara, with her large mouth and spiky red hair, but the result was so unflattering, she ripped it up. Then, for something to do, she borrowed a swimsuit from Barbara, who was about her size, and went for a long swim in the complex's big pool. Afterward she stretched out on a lounge chair and fell asleep in the sun. She awoke with a burn on her back that bothered her all the way home to her mother's condo that afternoon.

Sunday evening Mom had another date with her personal trainer.

Tess found Ria in the guesthouse playing her recorder to the cat, who lay on the bed and didn't appear to be listening. When Tess curled up beside him, he raised his head and pushed against her hand. She petted him, and he licked her hand as if he were glad to see her. It made her feel calm and peaceful to lie there listening to the wistful sound of the recorder and the cat's purring.

The next morning Tess still couldn't find anything to eat in Mom's pantry. Mom should have stopped at a supermarket on their way back from Phoenix Sunday afternoon, but she hadn't thought of it. Neither of them had. Tess sighed, imagining the big breakfast Blair or Dad would have fixed. Sometimes it would be French toast or scrambled eggs, along with cereal and juice. This morning Tess was hungry enough to salivate at just the thought of such a meal. She and Mom had skipped supper last night. But usually Tess didn't care what she ate. She'd snack on whatever was around without really tasting it and be satisfied with frozen meals zapped in the microwave.

Dad and Blair made a big thing out of everyone sitting down to dinner together, even when their jobs kept them working late. At the table, they'd quiz each kid about how the day had gone. The adults reported as well, but never with any real problems. Tess had kind of enjoyed knocking holes in the ritual by announcing she'd gotten a D or had been given detention. Blair would look upset and her eyes would go to Brian and Annie. Tess, as the oldest, was failing to be an example to them again. When her father had pointed that out to her, she'd suggested they leave her out of the nightly dinner table quiz. "I hate it anyway," she'd said. But Dad had just looked pained and let her continue being a bad example. No question that hunger pangs were easier to deal with than that kind of stuff.

Mom staggered by on her way to the bathroom.

"I need a note to get on the bus, Mom," Tess said.

Mom grunted and disappeared for fifteen minutes. When she came back out, she said, "What should I say? I can't think at all this morning. My brain's dead. I shouldn't have stayed out so late last night." She took the pen and paper

Tess handed her and wrote as Tess dictated that she was living with her now and returning to school here. "You think that'll do it?"

"I guess," Tess said. She was pretty sure the bus driver would accept anything she handed to him, at least if it was the same bored young man who drove this route when she'd been on it last year.

"I may be late tonight, and I still haven't had a chance to stop at the supermarket," Mom said. "You could order in a pizza for dinner and invite your friend Ria if you want."

"Thanks. That sounds good," Tess said.

"You know," Mom said, eyeing Tess's rumpled attire disapprovingly, "we ought to get you some decent clothes. I'm already tired of seeing you in T-shirts and shorts."

"That's all I own, Mom."

"Umm." Her mother nodded. "Soon as I can, I'll take you shopping. I'm surprised Blair hasn't done that already."

"She wanted to, but I wouldn't let her."

"Oh? Well, it's true her taste is ultra-conservative."

"Her taste isn't so bad," Tess said defensively. "Only her style's not my style."

Mom smiled. "Boring's her style."

"She's smart, though."

Mom sniffed. "If you like her so much, how come you're here?"

Her mother had a point. Tess was defending Blair just to be contrary. "Because I like you better, Mom," she said to placate her mother. But not about clothes, Tess thought. A shopping trip with Mom was usually a disaster. Accent whatever you've got that's attractive was Mom's philosophy of dressing, whereas Tess liked clothes that helped her blend in with other kids her age.

"So will I see you tonight?" Tess asked.

"I don't know. Depends," Mom said. "I go to the health club after work and then— Look, Tess, I didn't expect you to be here during the week."

"I know, I know." But she had hoped to have time to talk to her mother.

Mom got up to leave. "Well, make the most of your day," she said. Already she was looking more like her dynamic self, ready to take on the business world and wow the clients.

"You'll call me if you're not coming home, then?" Tess asked.

"No," Mom said in annoyance. "I won't call you. You'll see me when I get here. . . . Don't torture your teachers too much the first day, huh?" She blew a kiss rather than risk smearing her carefully applied lipstick. "Where's my sample case?" she asked herself. As soon as she located it, she was out the door.

Tess ambled into her mother's bedroom and lay down on the mussed bed, but she didn't feel sleepy even with the familiar comfort of her mother's perfume on her sheets. She sat up and solemnly stared at the plain-faced girl with tangled shoulder-length hair that she saw in the mirror. Sighing, Tess used her mother's brush to make her hair into a neater frame around her face. Then she tucked in her T-shirt and found a belt from her mother's closet that would fit her. Mom's waist was a size smaller than hers. With the belt and the combed hair, Tess felt well enough dressed for school and she set off for the bus stop.

"Hi." Ria greeted her with a big smile. "It's like old times."

"Yeah. How did the cat do?"

"He slept on my stomach the whole night," Ria boasted.

Tess grunted unhappily. "And did you name him?"

"No yet. How about Mugsy?"

"Ugh."

"Or Silver?"

"Yuck."

The bus came. The driver said to Tess, "Not you again?"

"Hey, I'm back! Aren't you glad to see me? I was living with my father during the week, but now I'm home with my mother."

"Just what I need," the driver said. He frowned at her. "You better watch your step, kiddo. No smart-mouth remarks. No seat hopping. No tricks."

"Got you," Tess said. She gave him a friendly wink. He hadn't even wanted to see her note.

It was harder when she walked into Ria's homeroom and

found herself facing her old enemy. Mrs. Blythe used to be a substitute teacher, but she had a full-time job teaching seventh-grade math now.

"What are *you* doing here?" Mrs. Blythe demanded the instant she spotted Tess.

"Moved back with my mother. How are you, Mrs. Blythe?"

"Do you have transfer papers? Let me see them."

"What papers?"

"Before you can enter my class, I need official word from the office."

Tess showed her the note Mom had scrawled. Mrs. Blythe raised an eyebrow and sent her to see the principal.

Tess was indignant. Here she was subjecting herself to an eternity of boredom, and instead of being welcomed back, she was being treated like an alien invader. She sat in the principal's office half the morning waiting to speak to him. When the secretary finally sent her in, she let him have it full blast.

"What's the matter with you guys in this school? Don't you know it's your duty to educate me? I'm a minor. Why are you giving me grief after I show up voluntarily?"

"Sounds as if you haven't changed, Tess," he told her. "You've still got that attitude problem. We'll need your mother to fill out some forms. Also we'll need records from the school you were enrolled in before we can re-instate you here. But—" He gave her his blue-eyed laser look. "The first time you cause a riot in the cafeteria or lead an insurrection anywhere, you're in deep trouble. Understand?"

She understood. She had a record. They weren't about to cut her any slack. "I've matured since sixth grade," she assured him. "I won't get in any trouble."

"You'd better not. I won't tolerate having my teachers marching in here to complain that you won't do what you're told. Until then, good luck behaving yourself." He held out his large, fleshy hand. He was a big, balding man and he could be either very nice or very mean. Tess actually kind of liked him. She shook his hand and smiled at him.

"Well," he said. "You can attend classes the rest of the day as a visitor. Your friend Ria's in lunch right now. Just follow her around and remember how mature you've gotten."

She found Ria at a table of both boys and girls. She was sitting next to Gunther. It made Tess feel odd to be the only unpaired person at the table, but she tried not to let it show.

"So what've *you* been up to lately, Tess?" one of the boys who knew her from sixth grade asked with a grin. "You get kicked out of your new school?"

"No, I decided I like it better here."

"Why? Didn't you get along there?"

"I got along fine. They didn't expect everybody to be from the same cookie cutter like they do here in the country."

"You mean we're hicks?" Gunther asked her.

"I didn't say that."

"Hey, Tess!" A flying figure landed on the bench beside her with a thump. "You're back. For good?"

It was Al, who'd been her trouble-making partner in sixth grade. Between the two of them they had led the famous insurrection that the principal had mentioned. It hadn't been much, to Tess's way of thinking, just a conga line of kids escaping out the side door from a boring late-afternoon assembly. Tess had thought it was funny, especially the open mouth of the lecturer who was talking about safety in the home.

"Yeah. I'm back for good. How've you been, Al?"

"Okay. Listen, we've got this great idea and you're just who we need."

"No," she said.

"No what?"

"No. I can't. If I get in any trouble, I'm out of here before I start. They've already warned me."

"But Tess, this is going to be so cool. We've got this can of hairspray, see, and what we're going to do—"

"Don't tell me." She raised her hand in a stop signal. "I might be called in as a witness, and you know I can't lie."

"You can't?" Al looked surprised.

"No, I can't." That wasn't quite the case, Tess realized. She'd lie to make someone feel better or to make a good case for herself, as with the woman who'd given her a ride on the highway. But she didn't consider herself a liar, at least not when things were going well for her.

"Wow," Al said. "You sure have changed."

"I never lied before," she said. "That's why I got in so much trouble."

Riding back to the empty condo on the bus, Tess felt gloomy. It might not be as easy as she'd thought, staying with her mother and going to school with Ria. She wouldn't have to worry about rules at home, sure. But she'd be bound and gagged while she was in school. That was the reverse of her situation living with her father and Blair.

Besides, she didn't know if she could stand seeing Ria with *her* cat, especially if the cat was going to sleep on Ria's belly and follow her around.

"So are you glad to be back?" Ria turned from the window to ask her.

"I don't know," Tess said honestly.

Chapter 11

Tess had always been able to talk her heart out to her friend, but now Ria hardly seemed to listen to her. She was obsessed with Gunther. Ria had spent an hour—Tess had clocked her—discussing whether Gunther's over-protective mother would allow him to bike to Ria's house once school ended and he couldn't go home on the school bus with her anymore. With barely a breath between subjects, Ria had then speculated on whether she could teach Gunther to dance over the summer so that he could take her to eighth-grade parties.

Worse yet, Ria threw booby-trapped questions at Tess, like did she think Gunther's interest in lizards and his lack of interest in much else besides basketball made him a weirdo. In the kitchen Tuesday after school, Ria asked, "Do you think Gunther's cute?"

Tess had had it. "Can't you talk about anything but Gunther?"

"You're jealous that I've got a boyfriend, aren't you?" Ria said. "I was afraid you would be eventually."

"I'm not jealous. Believe me, I don't even want a boyfriend."

"Why not?"

"Because it makes you waste your time worrying about dumb things," Tess said.

"What's the matter with you, Tess?" Ria asked. "It never used to bother you when I talked about boys."

"You never talked about a boy and nothing else," Tess snapped.

"Well, I can't help it. And if you don't like it, you don't have to hang out here anymore," Ria said. Her normally pale face was flushed and her eyes were brimming.

"Fine with me," Tess shot back, and she stomped out of Ria's house.

Once she was alone in her mother's condo, she huddled into a simmering ball of misery. Mom was too busy with her own life to spare much time for her. Even the cat wasn't available as often as Tess needed him. She wanted someone to commune with . . . but who? She squatted in front of her mother's dresser and rested her chin on her crossed arms. Staring into the mirror, Tess dumped her thoughts onto the sullen-faced girl there.

"You *are* jealous, but not about Ria's boyfriend. It's that she has your cat. Because the cat picked *you*. He's *your* cat, not Ria's. You've just got to get him back somehow." Making the decision relieved her. Now all she had to do was figure out how to do it.

At the bus stop the next morning Ria said, "Sorry I gave you a hard time yesterday. I didn't mean it, Tess."

"That's okay," Tess said. "I didn't mean whatever I said, either." They smiled at each other and that ended the fight.

The next afternoon the two of them were snacking on cookies and grapes and chocolate milk in Ria's kitchen when Tess asked, "Where's the cat?"

"We leave him in the guesthouse during the day so he won't get in any trouble."

"You lock him up all day?"

"I don't think he minds, Tess. Mostly he sleeps, anyway."

"Did you name him yet?" Tess asked.

"Not yet. What do you think of Snoozy?"

"Yuck! He's not one of the seven dwarfs."

"I can't believe he doesn't have a name yet," Ria said. "How about I open the dictionary and close my eyes and point to a word?"

"No. He's got a name. We just have to find it."

Ria shrugged. "Okay. So you want me to go get him?"

Tess nodded, her mouth full of cookie. Ria ran out to the guesthouse and returned with the cat cuddled in her arms. "He was asleep on the pillow," she said.

The cat blinked his green eyes sleepily at Tess. "Hi, Cat," she said. "Remember me?"

Ria plopped him onto her lap. The cat promptly jumped off. Sitting in the middle of the kitchen floor, he began to groom himself. "You can tell he really misses me," Tess said glumly. She got down on the floor and reached out to stroke him. He backed away and resumed licking his chest.

"Hey, I thought we were friends!" Tess cried.

Ignoring her dismay, the cat finished his grooming and strolled into the living room as if he owned it. He jumped up on the windowsill and stared out into the courtyard. Doves were pecking at the crumbs Ria's mother had put out for them.

"Maybe he's mad at me because I gave him away," Tess said.

"He's just a cat," Ria said. "Cats aren't loyal like a dog is."

"But he followed me all the way from Catalina State Park, Ria."

"Yeah. But he's pretty comfortable here, so he doesn't need you anymore. . . . So what do you want to do? Watch TV?"

"There's nothing on in the afternoon," Tess said. What she wanted to do was woo the cat, but if she showed how devastated she was by his lack of interest in her, Ria would think she was crazy. "You have any new CDs?" Tess asked.

"I've got one by that singer you like—the one with the droopy clothes."

They listened to music, singing along with their favorite pop tunes. After a while Tess picked up the cat and stroked him. He tolerated that only until Tess released her hold on him. Then he leaped to the floor and sauntered off. Tess was crushed.

Ria's mother got home from work and announced, "We've got barbecued chicken for supper. Want to stay, Tess?"

"No. Thanks. I think I'll just go home," Tess said.

"What's the matter with you?" Ria asked.

"Nothing." Tess was embarrassed to admit that she was feeling blue because the cat didn't care about her anymore.

"See you tomorrow, Ria," Tess said at the door. She looked down and there was the cat at her heels ready to follow her.

"Don't let him out," Ria said in alarm.

"No. I won't." Tess gently pushed the cat away and slipped outside. But she felt much more cheerful walking home. At least the cat had tried to be with her. He hadn't forgotten her completely. Given the chance, he'd still choose her over Ria.

For the next hour, Tess put on one of her mother's exercise videotapes and bounced around the living room to its high-energy music. Her supper was an abandoned jar of salsa and some stale crackers. She felt lonesome, but not for Ria's company, not even for Mom's. "Ria has to share that cat with me," Tess told herself. That wasn't too much to ask of a good friend who'd just been given the pet she'd always longed for, was it?

The phone rang. "There you are," her father said. "I called you earlier. Where were you?"

"At Ria's."

"And where's your mother? Is she home from work yet?"

"Not yet, Dad. How are you?"

"Okay. I rented a Disney movie for the kids. They're watching it. Blair went to a Planned Parenthood meeting."

"I bet the house is pretty quiet without me around."

"Right. And how are you and your mother doing?"

"Fine. We always get along okay. She does her thing, and I do mine."

"Yes, I know—you're like two adults living together. But you're not an adult yet. You're a child and someone should be taking care of you. How's school going?"

"Okay. I've been on probation since my first day there, so I'm kind of having to behave myself."

"And you are? Behaving yourself?"

"Sure. I can walk the line when I have to."

"Then why couldn't you do that here?" he asked.

"Because you and Blair want me to be perfect," Tess said. "I'm happier here, Dad. That is, I would be if I had my cat back. He's sort of getting attached to Ria now that she's keeping him at her house."

Bitterly her father complained, "You act like you care more about that cat than your family."

"What family? You and Mom aren't married anymore."

"You have a family here with your sisters and Brian and Blair and me."

"They're yours, Dad, not mine."

"Tess, why must you be so unreasonable? You have to accept what is. You can't make things over to suit yourself." He sounded frustrated.

"So how is Annie?" Tess asked to soothe him. "Does she still talk about me?"

"She says you don't like princess videos."

"I don't. She's right. Is that what you got them?"

"No, she didn't want one because *you* don't like them. I got the one about the Dalmatians."

"Oh, yeah."

"This weekend Blair and I are planning to take the kids to the zoo to see that South American exhibit. Will you come?"

"Sure, I like zoos."

"Good," he said "I'll pick you up Saturday morning— say, around nine?"

"Could I bring the cat to your house? I mean, just to show Annie."

"You want me to be sneezing and miserable, Tess?"

"Maybe you wouldn't be so allergic to this one. There was a kid I knew once who had a cat he wasn't allergic to, even though he was allergic to most other cats."

"I don't want to risk it."

"Okay, okay. See you Saturday." Tess suspected Ria

wouldn't want her to take the cat visiting, anyway. Joint custody—that was what she had to work out with Ria, joint custody for the cat.

The personal trainer with the bulging arm muscles came in with Mom when she got home at ten that night. He was carrying four bags of groceries at once.

"Teddy, this is my daughter, Tess," Mom said.

"Hi, Tess." He extended a hand on an arm hung with two shopping bags and she shook it. His smile was sweet and his grip was firm and warm, but his baby face made him look younger than Mom had said. Tess thought he could even be a teenager.

"So you into any sport?" Teddy asked, cracking his knuckles while Mom put the groceries away.

"I'm a couch potato," Tess said. "What are you into *besides* sports?"

He smiled and jerked his eyebrows up and down in a way that was supposed to be humorous. "Beautiful women, practical jokes, money. What are you into?"

"Not much," Tess said. "I'm kind of a boring person."

"Yeah? Your mother says you're an original."

"An original what?"

"An original pain in the neck," Mom said. She poured out three glasses of fruit punch and put them down on the low table in front of the couch. "You want to go shopping in Nogales with Teddy and me on Saturday?"

"Sure," Tess said. "Can I bring my cat?"

103

"I thought you gave the cat to Ria."

"I did, but he's still partly my cat. We're going to share."
Ria didn't know that yet, but that was how it had to be.

"No cats in my car," Mom said.

"She hates cats," Tess told Teddy.

"I'm not too crazy about them myself," he said. "So you got any dance music?" he asked Mom

She smiled and said, "You bet."

Tess could tell by the way they were looking at each other that she ought to get out of the way, but where could she go? Her mother's bedroom? She'd be trapped in there until Teddy left, which might be hours. And she couldn't go to sleep in the living room until they cleared out of it. "Maybe I'll go down and see what Ria's up to," Tess said.

"It's after ten," Mom said.

Tess thought fast. "I'm sleeping in her guesthouse tonight with my cat."

"Oh, okay," Mom said without further questions. No doubt she would be glad to have Tess gone.

The cat wasn't in the guesthouse. It was probably already asleep on Ria's stomach. Disappointed, Tess lay down on the bed, meaning to nap for an hour or two and then go back home. Tomorrow she would have to call her father and tell him she couldn't go to the zoo with him after all because she was going to Nogales with her mother. He wouldn't like that. Well, too bad. He'd taken on a new wife and kids without asking how *she* liked it.

"Ria," Tess said at the bus stop the next morning, "I slept in your guesthouse last night."

"How come? You get mad at your mother?"

"No. But she was using the living room and I couldn't go to bed. Listen, how about if I sleep in the guesthouse sometimes and you let the cat sleep with me? That way he won't forget me."

Ria frowned. "But he's my cat, Tess. You gave him to me."

"Not for keeps. We're sharing him."

"We are? Since when? I don't want a part-time pet. He's either mine or— Anyway, Tess, you can't have him. Neither of your parents will let you keep him."

"But I was the one who found him. He followed me. He picked me."

Ria shrugged. "He likes me just as much as you now."

"Ria, it's not fair."

"What's not fair? You gave him to me."

"But I didn't mean to. I love that cat." The passion in her voice surprised her.

"You love him?" Ria sounded surprised, too.

"Yes," Tess said, although the admission made her feel naked.

Ria grew thoughtful. She looked up at the sky and down the street at the bus that was coming toward them. "I've got to think about it," she said.

Chapter 12

Tess suspected that her principal's strict-behavior format was dulling her brain. Even so, it was hard not to blurt out objections in class—and she had lots of them: having to use only blue or black pens, leave margins, show the steps in answering a math problem, not wearing flip flops or sandals without a strap in the back, not running in the halls. Plus she actually liked the seventh-grade teachers better at the middle school she'd attended near Blair's house. They spoke in livelier voices. They provoked classroom discussions. They even joked now and then. It hadn't been half as difficult for her to be good there as it was here in her old school.

Tess spent the morning brooding about the tyranny she was enduring. Meanwhile, Ria must have been thinking over the cat situation, because at lunchtime she relented.

"I guess you could sleep with the cat a couple of nights a week. But he'll still be mine."

"Okay!" Tess said eagerly. "Can I come over tonight? I need a cat-purr fix bad."

"Yeah. He does have a nice rumbly purr, doesn't he?" Ria said with a grin.

"Maybe we should call him Rumbly," Tess said.

"Mmm," Ria said. "Rumbly's not bad. But it's still not right. You know?"

"I know," Tess said. "Like Rumpelstiltskin, this cat has a name. We just have to guess it."

Ria nodded. One reason they got along so well was that they often thought alike.

Tess was so exuberant about getting partial custody of the cat that she forgot the restrictions on her behavior. When the social studies teacher told her to wake up and pay attention, she blurted out, in front of the whole class, "But your droning puts me to sleep."

He looked as if he'd like to kill her and advised her to prop her eyelids open and listen anyway, because there'd be a quiz Friday on today's lesson. Her classmates turned as one and glared at her.

"Like the quiz was my fault," Tess complained to Ria in the hall on their way to health.

"It was," Ria told her. "He never gives quizzes, just big unit tests."

Tess grunted. One little misstep and she had fallen into

it up to her hips. It wasn't fair. "How about we call the cat Max?" she said.

"Nah. But Gunther thinks we should call him by a boy's name like James or Henry."

"What does Gunther know about cats? He's a lizard person," Tess said.

"How about Gato? That's cat in Spanish," Ria said. "That was my mother's suggestion."

"Maybe I'll ask *my* mother."

"We could put all the names on pieces of paper and let the cat step on one."

"If we could find some good names—but we haven't yet," Tess said.

It was Gunther's afternoon to go home with Ria. He sat with her on the bus while Tess sat alone in the back. She refused to stop at Ria's house with them as they swung down the street past the emptied garbage cans. "I'll see you later, when I come for the cat," Tess said and continued to her mother's condo.

There she found Mom's one and only cookbook. Mom had inherited it from her mother. It was yellowed and brown-spotted and hadn't been opened in the four years since Grandma's death. Tess sat down to study it. If she didn't want to continue living on pizza and peanut butter, she had better learn to cook.

Thanks to the food shopping Mom had finally done, the contents of the refrigerator matched pretty well with one recipe for vegetable salad. Tess got to work. Her mother was thrilled when she got home to find the table set and a bowl of beans, onions, and boiled potatoes in a light vinaigrette sauce ready to eat.

"Tess, where did you learn to cook?"

"It's not hard, Mom. You just follow directions. It's like running a dishwasher or something."

They had hot dogs to go with the vegetable salad, which Mom said was yummy. Tess felt proud of the first meal she'd produced on her own. "So did you have fun with Teddy last night?" she asked her mother.

"Teddy's always fun. Why else would I bother with him? Incidentally, I told him that I was going on a business trip next week, and he offered to move in to keep you company." She held her hand up to halt the objection Tess had opened her mouth to make. "Don't worry," Mom said. "I told him no, that you were fine alone. And if you weren't, you could stay at your girlfriend's house."

"Good. Teddy's practically a stranger," Tess said. "And kids aren't supposed to talk to strangers—much less live with them."

"Of course not," Mom said. "Besides, it would be hard to get rid of Teddy if we let him move in. He doesn't earn much and he's always on the lookout to save money. No way do I want to end up supporting him."

"Where are you going on your business trip?"

"Florida. They want me to break in a new sales manager in Orlando."

Tess was wondering what she would do with herself for

a week alone in the condo. Sketch? Watch TV? It occurred to her that she could bring the cat over once her mother was gone. After all, Mom wasn't allergic the way Dad was.

"So we'll go shopping for whatever you think you'll need," Mom was saying, "and then if you have any kind of emergency, you can call your father or Ria. I'll leave you with enough money to call for a taxi if worst comes to worst. You should be okay, huh?" Mom didn't look too certain.

"I'll be fine. But don't tell Dad you're going for the whole week."

"Right. He'd worry, wouldn't he? I mean, if you go by age, you're not old enough to be on your own. But you're more sensible than any eighteen-year-old I've known."

"Thanks." Tess was pleased with the compliment. At least her mother appreciated how mature she was, even if no one else in her life did.

Something was wrong at Ria's house. As Tess stood in the courtyard outside her friend's front door, she could hear Ria's father yelling about "not being made of money." She hesitated. Should she just slip into the guesthouse and wait a while? Or should she ring the doorbell and hope that an outsider's presence would shut him up? She rang the doorbell.

Nobody answered. She rang again.

The door flew open. "Whaddaya want?" Ria's father asked. He looked like a thunderhead, a dark gray one fixing to storm.

"It's me, Ria's friend, Tess."

"I know who you are. You're the one who stuck us with that cat. Well, you can take it back right now."

"Daddy!" Ria cried from somewhere behind him. "Please! You said I could have a pet. You said . . . Don't make me give the cat back to Tess."

"I keep telling you," her father roared over his shoulder at Ria, "we got to cut down. All you and your mother do is spend, spend, spend."

"Mom's returning the clothes. She said she'd take them back tomorrow."

"That's not all she's going to take back." He shut the door in Tess's face and began yelling for his wife.

Tess retreated to a bench on her mother's patio. Yelling like that shook her. Dad never raised his voice and Mom rarely did. Besides, even when Mom shouted, she wasn't scary. Tess thought she'd better keep out of sight and not make Ria's father any angrier. But what if he were serious about not letting Ria keep the cat? Then what? The cat must be welcome someplace. The trouble was Tess couldn't think of where.

"Your father was really mad last night," Tess said the next morning when she saw Ria at the bus stop.

"Yeah. The bar's not making money like he expected, and he's scared he might lose his lease. He always yells when things don't work out for him. That's the only time my mother shuts up, when Dad yells. But don't tell anyone,

Tess. Mom hates having people know our family business."

"I won't tell," Tess said again, although it struck her as odd that Ria's mother was so inquisitive about other people's lives and so secretive about her own. "So what about the cat? Did your father mean it about not letting you keep him?"

"I don't know. Sometimes he forgets. Mom'll take back the summer clothes she bought us—except for a couple of pairs of shorts; mine don't fit anymore—and then we'll see."

"But your mother earns her own money, doesn't she?"

"Not much. She only works part-time. Plus he makes her put it into their joint account. Then he writes all the checks. That way he can watch how much we have."

"What if I pay for the cat's food and litter stuff?"

"Yeah. I could tell him you'd do that. But it might make him mad. I mean, he's funny about money. He hates not having it and he hates not earning enough. But once when his brother offered him money, he got insulted and wouldn't talk to him for a year."

"Well, I can't keep the cat," Tess said. "The only other thing I can think of is to take him back to where he found me so he can pick someone else to adopt him . . . if he doesn't get eaten by a coyote first."

"Maybe someone in school would take him."

"Who'd adopt a full-grown cat? And besides, Ria, I don't want to give him to anybody else."

"No. Me, neither. So . . ." Ria thought. "Let's hope my father forgets what he said."

Tess nodded, but she believed Ria's father had meant his threat and wouldn't forget.

"And don't say anything to my mother," Ria said. "Like you're not supposed to know about the lease or anything."

"I know."

They got on the bus and set their minds on school business.

That was the day Gunther brought his live lizard collection to science class. He had five different kinds, including a horny toad that looked like a dragon and sat in his hand so peacefully that Tess had to admit it was cute. The lizard collection was a big success and Gunther was star of the show. Ria decided he wasn't such an oddball, after all. She even let him hold her hand in the hall where everyone could see them. Watching them together, Tess felt lonely. A boyfriend might not be such a bad idea, she thought. But looking around her classes, she didn't see a boy whose hand she wanted to hold. The cat was the only truly lovable creature she knew, besides her parents and Ria.

Mom was supposed to leave for her Florida business trip on Monday morning. On Thursday night she asked Tess if she wanted to spend the weekend with her father, as planned. "Or would you rather go to a dude ranch with Teddy and me?"

"The dude ranch, for sure," Tess said.

"It's Teddy's uncle's ranch. He invited us because business is kind of slow right now. You and I could bunk together. We'll stay overnight and come back on Sunday."

"Uh-huh." Tess guessed bunking with her daughter would give Mom an excuse not to share a room with Teddy. "So how will Teddy feel about that?"

"If he doesn't like it, we don't have to go. I'm not that crazy about horses, anyway."

It was Tess's father who objected when she called him about it. "You haven't seen me in two weeks, Tess. Blair and I were planning things that you, especially, might enjoy. I mean, besides the zoo."

"Well . . . but a dude ranch, Daddy." She thought of telling him she could come visit him for the whole of next week, then remembered that it would upset him to know that her mother was leaving her alone in the condo. Besides, a week out of school wouldn't be too smart when she'd only just started back here.

"I suppose I can't compete with anything as glamorous as a dude ranch," her father said in a leaden voice. "We're going for a picnic in Sabino Canyon. I thought you and I could get in a short hike together."

"Dad, I do want to be with you, really," Tess said. "I mean, if it was just you and me . . . Remember our camping trips?"

"I saw the pictures you drew of them," he said stiffly.

"You found those sketches? I was saving them to give you for Father's Day. How did you find them?"

"When Blair and I were looking for clues as to where you'd run away to," he said.

"You poked around the stuff in my room? My private stuff?" Tess was shocked.

"It was an emergency," Dad said. "You were gone and I was frantic."

"But you didn't have any right——"

"Tess, let's not argue. You were gone without warning, and I had to get you back somehow. Now, let me speak to your mother."

"She's out right now."

"Again? When is she ever home?"

"Dad, I'm doing fine here. My only problem is the cat. Ria has him, but her father doesn't like him, and if he won't keep him, I don't know what to do. And no, I'm not taking the cat to an animal shelter."

"Did I say you should?"

"Well, I'm stuck for ideas."

He hesitated. "I'll think about it."

"Thanks," she said. She didn't expect he'd come up with anything she'd be willing to accept—but then again, he might. The cracks in the concrete of his personality sometimes held surprises, like the way he could be so relaxed and wise about the natural world on a campout. Her heart warmed to him then, but not when she was living with him and he was telling her what to do or criticizing her. Probably that was why she felt so much more comfortable around her mother, because her mother took her as she was.

Chapter 13

Tess had fun on the dude ranch that weekend, although she didn't spend much time with her mother. Mom would only go trail riding for an hour Saturday morning. The rest of the time, she and Teddy hung out at the pool, showing off their great bodies and getting a tan. Meanwhile Tess took off with the wranglers and three paying guests for a four-hour trail ride up a steep canyon. She saw mule deer and a bumpy toad that made her think of Gunther. Bright red and yellow flowers of prickly pear cactus and cholla splashed against the brown of the mountains and the sapphire sky. The beauty exhilarated her and the steady rocking of her horse lulled her.

"It was fabulous," she told her mother at supper that night as they ate a huge meal of barbecued chicken and grilled vegetables.

"More fun than being with your father and Blair?" Mom asked.

"Lots more," Tess said, which made both her mother and Teddy laugh.

Tess's thighs ached after the long ride, but she soaked in the hot tub that night and went out on an early-morning ride Sunday.

"I didn't know you were still so keen on horses," Mom said.

"Yeah. If I can ever get some riding lessons, I could become a wrangler when I grow up."

Mom groaned and said, "Maybe I should have let you go to the zoo with your father."

"Then she might have wanted to be a lion tamer," Teddy pointed out.

He was in high spirits as they headed home in Mom's car Sunday afternoon. He sang and joked, obviously proud of himself for having provided them with such fine entertainment. Mom still wasn't letting him get too cozy with her, though. She packed her bag for her business trip and then kicked him out of the condo before ten that night. "I've got to get a good night's rest before I leave tomorrow," she told him when he protested.

In the morning Mom gave Tess the telephone number of the hotel in Orlando where she'd be staying. "You sure you're okay being alone in the condo until Friday night?" she asked again. "Maybe you should go stay with Ria."

"I'll be fine," Tess said. She had plenty to eat. She had

school to keep her busy. Ria was there if she needed her. And best of all, the cat would be there to keep her company. For a change he could sleep on *her* stomach.

She did feel a little strange, though, when she got home after school Monday afternoon knowing her mother was in Florida by now. Tess wandered through the three rooms, opened her mother's drawers, fingered her flimsy silk underwear. She even tried on a couple of simple-looking shifts from Mom's walk-in closet. The shifts fit, but whereas her mother gave them a distinctly female shape, they hung like paper bags on Tess. Her features were okay, she decided, studying them in the mirror—eyes, nose, and mouth regular, and neither too big nor too little. But her hair was fly-away wavy, and the total effect was sort of blah. Mom was a knockout. Tess was purely crowd-scene material. She made faces at herself in the mirror and advised her image that since she wasn't downright ugly she shouldn't complain.

In a little while she walked down to Ria's house and asked for the cat. "I can keep him at the condo this whole week while my mother's gone," she said.

"Good," Ria said. "I hid him in the guesthouse this weekend, out of Dad's way, but he knocked over the lamp and scratched the door. If either of my parents see it, I'm in trouble."

"This cat likes his freedom," Tess said. "You want to come over to the condo? You could spend the night with me, too."

"Wait here and I'll ask Mom."

Tess waited five minutes. She was wondering what her friend was doing when Ria finally came back with the cat, and a plastic bag with kitty litter, a pan, and a poop strainer. "Mom wants me to stay home with her tonight," Ria said.

"Why?"

Ria shrugged. Her reluctance to answer meant it had something to do with her father again. "Okay," Tess said. She accepted the cat and his toilet equipment. "Thanks." She figured Ria's father must still be having difficulties.

Walking back up the street with the cat held against her chest, Tess said, "So Cat, you're all mine until Friday. Isn't that great?"

Ignoring her question, the cat braced himself as if he were awaiting a chance to leap and run. Tess kept a good grip on him. Once inside the condo, he seemed to relax and she set him down on the pull-out couch.

"If you want to look around, you're welcome," Tess said. She went to get some water for him and a can of tuna fish.

He followed her into the kitchen and brushed against her legs, then turned and brushed against her going back the other way. As soon as she reached down to pet him, he lifted his head into her hand and closed his eyes and kept pushing at her hand. When she sat down cross-legged in the middle of the tiny kitchen floor, he climbed into her lap and pushed his head against her body as hard as he could. All the while he was motoring away loudly.

"You're a real lover," she said. "Maybe we should call you Lovey."

He looked at her with wide green eyes, then climbed to her shoulder and jumped from there onto the kitchen counter. It didn't take him long to sniff his way through the kitchen, with a stop at the dish of tuna she'd set out. He sampled a bite of it and cruised back into the living room. What he fancied most, apparently, was Mom's queen-size bed. There he stretched out on his back in the very middle and rolled luxuriously from one side to the other.

"Well, look at you," Tess mocked him. He blinked sleepily at her with his eyes crossed and his tongue hung out, looking so silly she laughed out loud.

"Just don't get too used to it," she warned him, "because when Mom comes back, you're out of here."

And then what? Then maybe Ria's father would miss the cat and allow her to take him back to their house? Fat chance! But anything was possible with that moody man. Tess put on the exercise video and began working out to the thumping beat of the music. When she lay down for the floor exercises, the cat came and stood on her stomach. He peered at her face, his nose only a few inches from hers.

"What is it? You think I've gone crazy? Don't worry. This is normal people behavior."

He followed her to the bathroom when she took her shower and sat on the sink pawing at the drip from the faucet. When she got out of the shower, he meowed.

"You think the drip is too slow?" She increased the

stream for him. That intrigued him so much that he got down into the sink with both front paws to try to catch the water. His big green eyes got rounder and wilder.

"You're nutty, Cat. You know that?"

He knocked the toothpaste cap onto the floor and chased it around the toilet while she brushed her teeth. But when she turned off the light and left the bathroom, he was right at her heels, and he leaped onto her mother's bed before her. This time instead of sleeping on her stomach, he stretched out across her armpit with his head under her chin. She could feel his breath tickling her neck as she fell asleep.

Tuesday, when she got home from school, Tess saw a man in a car parked outside her mother's condo. She recognized him. It was Haig, the big dark-haired guy who had been Mom's live-in boyfriend, the one who'd scared Mom enough to make her change the front-door locks. Tess's heart began racing. She hesitated. Should she go in with him watching her? Then he'd know she had the key. It might not be such a good idea to have him know that, not if he wanted to get into the condo for some reason.

Turning on her heel, she hustled down the street to Ria's house and used the guesthouse key to let herself in. The cat would have to stay alone in Mom's condo for a while longer. Tess lay down on the bed wishing she had some music to listen to or a book to read. How long was that guy likely to wait for Mom? When her stomach told her it was near suppertime, she got up and walked back toward the condo. As soon as she saw that the car was still there, she reversed and ran back to Ria's and rang the door bell. Ria's mother answered.

"Hi," Tess said. "Is it okay if I hang out with Ria for a while?"

"Of course, Tess. Come on in. Ria's in her bedroom doing her homework. We're having supper in a few minutes. You're welcome to stay if you don't mind leftovers."

"Oh, you don't have to feed me," Tess said.

"It's no trouble—we have plenty of food," Ria's mother said. "Is your mother working late, or is she out on a date?"

"She's working," Tess said cautiously.

"She must worry having to leave you home alone in the evening. I never take a job that would keep me away from my family," Ria's mother said.

"Mom does her best," Tess said.

"I'm sure. And how's your father doing with his new wife?"

"Fine, I guess. She's a good cook, like you, and her kids are cute—sometimes . . . when they're not being pests."

"But you'd rather live with your mother?"

"Well, I like being near Ria," Tess said. Her partial truths just missed being lies.

Having satisfied some of Ria's mother's curiosity, Tess felt she'd paid her dues. "I guess I'll go see if Ria is finished with her homework."

She flopped on Ria's bed and told Ria about the man who was parked outside her mother's condo.

"That's scary," Ria said. "You better stay here tonight."

"I can't. The cat's alone there. What if he wrecks something in Mom's place? She doesn't know I've got him there."

They decided that after dinner Ria could go for a run past the condo and see if the car had left. Haig had never met Ria, so she'd be safe.

Ria's father came home in the middle of dinner. "Got hung up," he said pleasantly, and smiled in a friendly way at Tess. "Anything left for me to eat?" he asked his wife.

"Plenty," Ria's mother said. "I'll just pop it in the microwave so it's hot, the way you like it." She hesitated. "Did you have a good day?"

"Yeah." He slumped into his seat at the table. "An old buddy of mine came by. Said he might be able to help me out with the landlord. He's like that with the guy." Ria's father held up two crossed fingers. "I told him he's got free drinks coming the rest of his life if he can get the landlord to renew my lease."

"Oh, what good news!" Ria's mother said, and she actually clapped her hands in delight. For the rest of the meal, she chattered about the neighborhood man who was attacked by a pack of javelinas in his own garage, and about the old couple who'd lived in the development longer than anyone and were going to have to move into a retirement place now. Ria and Tess watched TV. Promptly at eight,

Ria said she needed some exercise and was going for a run.

"I don't want you going out alone at night," her father said.

"I'll go with her," Tess said.

She went, but stopped just out of sight of Ria's house and watched Ria dash up the street past her mother's condo. Ria was back in a minute, breathing hard.

"Is he still there?" Tess asked.

"No," Ria said. "There's no car near your house."

"Good. I'll go home and see what the cat's up to." But first she returned to Ria's house to say goodbye. Ria's mother and father were sitting on the couch watching television. They looked like such a normal couple that Tess found it hard to believe Ria's father could yell like a maniac. "Come back soon," her father said.

Alone in the dark, Tess shivered with nervousness as she fumbled with the key to the condo. What if that man was hiding somewhere watching? He could have parked the car out of sight and be looking in from the patio in back. It was a relief when she finally got the key to work and could slip into the condo and lock the door behind her. Her heart was still pounding as she flipped on the lights and ran to close all the blinds.

The cat meowed at her accusingly from the middle of the living room. It took Tess a while to satisfy his craving for attention. Finally she got out a ribbon from the utility drawer, tied a plastic twist onto it, and swung it in front of him. The cat didn't seem interested in playing with it, though. He was content to stand on her lap kneading her legs with his paws and meowing his complaints at her. She flipped on the TV. The cat lay on her lap while she watched comedy and cop shows until nearly midnight. By the time she turned off the TV, she had put her mother's old boyfriend out of her mind.

Then came the knock at the door. Tess caught her breath in terror. Who was it? It was too late for Ria to be knocking.

"Clare, it's Haig," came a deep male voice asking for Tess's mother. "I need to talk to you."

Tess swallowed. Too petrified to move, she stared at the door. Had she remembered to lock it?

"Clare, don't make me stand out here like this. Open the door. Come on."

Tell him her mother wasn't home? Not a good idea. He'd know she was alone in the house then, alone and unprotected. She switched the TV back on to hide his voice.

"Clare!" he shouted. "Please, I just want to—" His cursing came through clear over the sound of the TV. Tess thought about calling the police. But they'd take a while to get here. So would her father. Should she call Ria's house and ask if *her* father would come up? Tess chewed on her thumb. She got up finally and put her hand on the phone. Please go away, she begged silently. Go away and leave me alone.

After a while she didn't hear anything. Had he gone?

She turned off the TV and still didn't hear anything. The cat meowed around her ankles. "Shush," Tess said.

She listened at the door. No sound. And then she heard an engine revving up loudly and a car pulling away too fast. She took a deep breath. Why did her mother have to get involved with a man like that? Dad might be uptight and a fusspot, but he was always reasonable and never violent.

Tess drank some milk in the dark kitchen, afraid to turn on any lights in case Haig had been pretending and hadn't really gone away. Still in the dark, she peered out of every window in the condo without seeing much of anything. Finally she felt safe enough to go to bed. This time the cat kissed her goodnight. He tipped out his tongue and touched it delicately to her chin.

"Good night, Cat," Tess said with tearful gratitude. "I love you, too."

She held him lightly, but his rumble resounded inside her chest. It made her feel safe enough to fall asleep.

Chapter 14

Tess got to the bus stop before Ria for a change. She was watching one pencil-size lizard chase another into a dying patch of prickly pear when the car pulled up next to her and stopped. She jumped back when she saw who it was.

"Where's your mother?" Haig asked, leaning his big, craggy head toward her through his open window.

Cautiously Tess backed even farther out of his reach. If he made a move to open the door, she'd bolt and run. Where? Ria's house.

"Her car wasn't there last night. Did she leave you alone?"

"No," Tess said and lied quickly, "Mom's car's getting fixed."

"I need to talk to her. When does she get home from work?"

"The usual time," Tess stalled. "Sometimes. Sometimes she comes late."

"I just want to talk to her. You know who I am, don't you?"

"Sure," Tess said. She had first met Haig last fall on a day when Mom had forgotten to pick her up at Dad's house and Dad had driven Tess to the condo. When he had seen the black convertible parked next to Mom's car, Dad had frowned. He'd said that Mom must be having company and maybe they should come back later. Tess had assured her father that it was fine, just Mom's new boyfriend whom Tess was going to be introduced to that weekend. But when Tess had let herself into the unlocked condo, she'd walked into the middle of a fierce argument.

"You'd better leave, then, if you're going. My daughter's here," Mom had said to the guy.

He'd glowered at Tess and Mom hadn't introduced him. He would have been handsome if his face weren't set in such deep, grim lines, Tess had thought. Suddenly he'd marched out without saying goodbye.

When Tess had asked what he was mad at, Mom had said, "Haig's always mad at something. He wanted me to go to Vegas with him and I said I couldn't go this weekend." Shrugging as if it were of no importance, Mom had asked cheerfully, "So you ready for our great shopping trip?" And they'd gone to the mall without any further mention of Haig, although his belongings kept turning up in places that made it plain he lived in the condo, too.

"Is your mother seeing someone else?" Haig asked Tess now.

"Just a guy who doesn't matter to her," Tess said. Her heart was pumping blood so loudly she was afraid he might hear it.

"All right, then. You tell her she needs to listen to me. That's all, just listen to me. You'll tell her?"

"Yes," Tess said.

"I'll see you later, then." He gunned the engine and drove off. Tess sagged in relief.

"Who was that guy you were talking to?" Ria asked. She had come strolling up to the bus stop as Haig left.

Tess took a deep breath. "The one my mother changed the locks to keep out."

"Uh-oh! What did he want?"

"To see Mom . . . Ria, I can't go back to her condo today. Can I hang out in your guesthouse?"

"Sure."

"I'll go get the cat and put him there now."

"Here comes the bus," Ria said. "Get the cat after school. He'll be all right."

"That man scares me."

"Yeah, well, he must be pretty rotten if your mother changed the locks on him. Maybe you ought to call your father about him."

"And tell him Mom's gone on a business trip? He'd be mad at both of us."

"Well . . . but that guy," Ria said. "Wouldn't you

rather have your *father* mad at you? Your dad's so nice."

"Yes, he is," Tess agreed. She wondered what her father could do about her mother's ex-boyfriend. Whatever it was would be better than what she could do. Her only option was to hide from him.

They got on the bus and took seats midway to the back. Tess asked Ria about her father. "Did that guy who was going to help him with his landlord do it?"

"Dad finds out today."

"Oh."

They talked about sending Gunther to the condo to collect the cat, but Tess wasn't sure the cat would let Gunther pick him up. "Maybe you and Gunther could go with me. We'd be safe in a group," Tess said.

"Yeah, but what if your mother's old boyfriend's somewhere watching?" Ria said nervously. "I don't want him coming into my house in the middle of the night to get you."

Especially not if she was going to be alone in the guesthouse, Tess thought. "We'll think of how to do it," she said.

But they had no time to think up a good plan in school, and on the way home the best they came up with was Gunther's idea of disguising Tess as an exterminator and having her cart out the cat in a box. They couldn't agree on the right costume for her, though. That was just as well, because as it turned out they didn't need a plan. Dad was there when they got off the school bus. His mouth was turned down at the ends and Tess knew she was in trouble.

"Dad, how come you're here?"

"I called your mother's office to speak to her and discovered she's out of town. Why did you lie to me, Tess?"

"I didn't lie exactly. I just said—"

"What you *didn't* say was that you were staying at your mother's place alone."

"I wasn't alone. I have the cat with me."

He grunted with disgust. "Don't give me that garbage," he said. "Go pack your belongings. You're coming home with me, like it or not. I spoke to your mother in Florida, so she knows."

Tess looked at Ria and Gunther, who were listening in open-mouthed silence. "But what about the cat?" Tess asked.

"Didn't you give the cat to Ria?"

"She did," Ria said.

"Fine. Then Ria can take the cat to her house," Dad said. "Get in the car." His voice was so commanding that they all climbed into the back seat, even Gunther. Dad drove to the condo. Tess looked around but didn't see Haig's car.

"You going to tell your father about that guy?" Ria whispered to her while Tess was packing and Dad was listening, without much interest, to Gunther's lecture about how horny toads squirt blood from their eyes to scare off a predator.

"I might as well," Tess said. "He's mad at me and Mom

already, and I sure don't want that man coming when Mom's alone here, either."

"Right," Ria said.

The cat, which had been nowhere in sight when the four of them invaded the apartment, emerged from behind the TV just as Tess closed the zipper on her backpack.

"There you are," Tess said. "Come meet my father." She picked him up and approached her father, who backed away fast.

"No closer," Dad said. "I feel a sneeze coming on already." And to prove it he sneezed.

The cat flinched in Tess's arms. Sadly, she handed him over to Ria. This was it, then. "Goodbye, my puss-puss," Tess said in a heartbroken voice.

As if he understood her, the cat cried and strained to go to her, pushing his legs hard against Ria's confining arm.

"I can't keep you, Cat," Tess said. "I'm sorry, but I just can't."

"Come on," Dad said. "No more dramatics. Let's go."

Tess sent Gunther to the kitchen for the litter box and the cat food. Dad carried the backpack and Tess took the struggling cat from Ria's hands. The cat clung to Tess. It dug its claws in so hard that she yelped. Obviously he knew he was losing her. She disengaged his claws and carried him feet up, cuddled in her arms like a baby to Ria's house. There she said goodbye to Ria and Gunther while Dad waited in the car.

"Take good care of my cat," Tess said.

"Our cat," Ria corrected. But then she relented and added, "It's okay, Tess. When you visit your Mom, you'll see us. It's not like you're going away forever."

"I feel like I am," Tess said. "Dad'll never allow me to live with Mom full-time now." Tears were trickling down her cheeks despite her effort not to cry.

"How about calling him Meow?" Gunther said.

Both girls grimaced.

"It was just a suggestion," Gunther said mildly.

Tess dragged her feet out to her father's car. On the way home he lectured her nonstop about the dangers of living on your own at too young an age, and how she would just have to endure his paternal concern until she was at least eighteen. "And probably long past that, if you want to know the truth," he said. "I'm responsible for taking care of you. And I take my responsibilities seriously, whether you like it or not. Do you understand?"

"Daddy," she said. "I'm glad you came."

"You are?"

His surprise made her smile, even though she was still feeling bad. "Well, except that I had to leave the cat. But—" And she told him about Haig.

Dad drew in his breath. "I'd better call the police and ask them to keep an eye on the condo," he said. "And we'll speak to your mother in Orlando and warn her."

Tess nodded and relaxed.

Annie yelled, "Tessie!" the instant she saw her stepsister in the entry hall. She ran and jumped into Tess's arms, wrapping her legs around Tess and nearly knocking her off her feet. "I missed you," Annie said.

Tess hugged and kissed Annie. "Well, I'm back now. You want to play a game of Candyland after dinner?'

"No, now," Annie said.

"She can play Go Fish," Brian said. "I taught her. We could all three play Go Fish."

"Okay," Tess said agreeably. She noticed Blair standing there grinning at her and went over deliberately and hugged her stepmother. "I'm sorry I upset Dad," Tess said.

"You upset me, too," Blair said. "I didn't like to think you'd rather live alone than be with us."

"Oh, you guys aren't so bad," Tess said. "Just too fussy. And anyway, I had this cat, a really special cat. And my friend Ria. And my mom and I do get along pretty well."

"I'm sure you do. Look," Blair said, "how about we decide on a minimum list of rules you need to abide by, a bare minimum, the least we can all live with? We'll sit down together and write up a contract, okay?"

"Umm," Tess said dubiously. A contract sounded very orderly. And rules, no matter how few, were like prison walls.

"Meanwhile, it's good to have you back." Blair hugged her hard—the first time she'd ever done so without Tess's permission.

In the morning when Tess returned to her old seventh-grade class, the teacher didn't seem too thrilled to see her, but kids smiled at her on her way to the empty desk by the closet. Immediately a note was passed to her.

"We're going to turn in blanks on the student council nominations forms for next year. You with us?"

"No. I'll nominate me," Tess wrote back without thinking about it.

"Good idea," the note came back. "We'll all nominate you."

Tess grinned. That would really put the teacher's nose out of joint.

The school was only a four-block walk from Blair's house, the house that she and her first husband had bought just before he died. When Tess walked in that afternoon, Blair called to her from the room that she used as her office. "Your friend Ria wants you to call her. She says it's urgent."

Tess had been looking forward to raiding Blair's well-stocked refrigerator, but she called Ria instead. "What's up?"

"Dad came home mad last night. That guy who was going to help him didn't have any luck with the landlord. Dad's got to close the bar."

"I'm sorry," Tess said cautiously. "Was he really tearing mad?"

"Yeah. I was out in the guesthouse with the cat, playing my recorder, and he came out to see why I wasn't doing the dishes for Mom and he saw the scratches—I told you the cat scratched up the door pretty bad trying to get out? Well, I was holding the cat, but Dad's yelling scared him and he jumped out of my hands and ran out the door and we heard a car screech."

"What? A car? You mean the cat ran into the street?"

"Well, I don't know for sure. But when Dad and I looked for him, we didn't see anything—I mean, no cat, no car, nothing. It was pretty dark out and Dad wasn't done yelling at me. So . . . I'm sorry, Tess."

"You think the cat got hit?"

"I don't know, but we couldn't find him anywhere." Ria was crying hard now.

"Don't cry, Ria," Tess said automatically. "Maybe the car didn't even hit him. Maybe he's just hiding." She kept repeating that hope until Ria calmed down.

It was only after the phone call ended that Tess let herself feel sick. Then she walked right to her stepmother's office and knocked. "Blair?" she called through the closed door. "Could you help me?"

The door opened quickly. "What's wrong?" Blair asked.

Tess concluded her explanation of what had happened to the cat with, "I can't just leave him out there waiting for a coyote to eat him. I can't."

"Of course not," Blair said, her honey-brown eyes full of concern. "We'll go look for him. But Tess, if we don't find him—in, say an hour—we've got to come back home."

Tess nodded. She was desperate enough to be grateful for whatever help Blair was willing to offer.

Chapter 15

The first thing Blair did was to create some eye-catching "Lost Cat" posters on her computer. "What do you think?" Blair asked.

"Those look okay," Tess said.

Blair raised an eyebrow and waited as if she expected more. Tess gave her a puzzled stare until she realized Blair wanted her to say thank you. Three beats of silence later, Blair sighed and said, "I'll post these around your old neighborhood while you look for the cat."

"I come, too," Annie said.

"And me," Brian said quickly. "Annie and me are good finders."

"It's up to you, Tess," Blair said. "I could leave Brian and Annie with Mrs. Jackson and baby Sara."

"No, they can come with us," Tess said.

Brian and Annie squealed as if Tess had just invited them to a party. With her usual speed and efficiency, Blair got the three of them into her car and had them all in Tess's old neighborhood half an hour later.

"You two want to stay in the car to help me put up posters or go with Tess to look for the cat?" Blair asked her children.

"We want to go with Tess," Brian said. "Right, Annie?"

"With Tessie," Annie said with an emphatic nod of her head.

Tess led her exploration group around the outside of her mother's condo first. "Hey, Cat, it's me, Tess," she called. Somewhere, she imagined the cat hiding, hurt and alone, afraid that she'd deserted him. "Meow if you're here," Tess urged.

Brian laughed and meowed. Tess frowned at him. "It's not funny, Brian."

"I know," he said apologetically.

While Tess whistled and called and crept around the tiles of her mother's patio, peering under every flowering bush and behind every plant, Brian and Annie crawled after her, peering, too. They even checked inside her mother's condo, although Tess knew the cat couldn't have gotten in on its own.

"Cat, Cat, Cat!" Annie shouted in the middle of Mom's bedroom.

Tess had to tell her that yelling would just scare him

deeper into hiding. "The cat doesn't know you, Annie. You wouldn't go to a stranger who called you, would you?"

Annie shook her head solemnly. After that both she and Brian tiptoed around in silence.

Tess started leading them down the street to check around Ria's house, but Blair returned in the car before they got to it. Her timing was good. Annie was wilting like an unwatered flower.

"I tired," she told her mother.

"Get back in the car, then. You, too, Brian," Blair said.

The loss of her rescue party discouraged Tess. Not that they'd been much use, but their presence had buoyed her faith that the cat could be found. "I don't know where he would've holed up," Tess said anxiously to Blair.

"Where haven't you looked yet?" Blair asked as she latched Annie into her car seat again.

"Ria's property," Tess said with renewed hope. "He could be there."

Ria's mother stepped onto her back patio when she saw Tess prowling around the yard. "He's not here, Tess," she said. "I even went into the wash to look for him. Ria's daddy feels bad that he scared the cat, but he was so upset when he saw the scratches on the door. You can't blame him that the animal ran in front of a car."

Tess bit her lip, swallowing hard on her disagreement. "Well, if you see the cat . . ." she said.

"We'll keep him for you. But you'll have to find another home for him. Ria's daddy's having difficulties right now and so. . . . You know?"

Tess nodded to end the conversation and hurried back to the street. She walked up and down it, then up and down again, calling all the while. She explored every potential hiding spot, no matter how small. Blair trailed her in the car suggesting places where a small animal might hole up. But when Tess crouched in front of the storm sewer pipe that ran out into the wash, Blair called, "Don't go in there! You could run into a snake or a gila monster."

"But this would be a good place to hide," Tess said.

"Poke a stick in, if you want. Just you stay out," Blair insisted. "Wait! I'll find you a stick." She hopped out of the car, leaving Annie and Brian inside it, and plunged into the wash. Reluctantly Tess loitered by the car.

"Home," Annie cried, rubbing her eyes.

"Not yet," Brian told her. "We're still looking for Tess's cat."

The stick Blair returned with was a five-foot-long dried ocotillo cane. "Be careful, it's still got thorns," Blair said as she handed it over.

Tess swept the inside of the storm sewer with the thin branch without touching anything soft.

"Annie needs a nap bad, Tess, and I have to get back and let Mrs. Jackson go," Blair said.

"Just another few minutes," Tess begged.

"I'll give you ten. Then we leave. The signs should get some response tonight when people pass them on their way home from work."

Tess swallowed and hurried into the wash. She walked as far as she could by threading her way through cactus and creosote bushes and fountain grass, and calling and calling and calling until she was hoarse. If the cat had retreated to this landscape, a coyote had already eaten him, for sure. The few natural hiding places were either holes in the ground or tangles of dead prickly pear where pack rats nested. The thorny plants provided little shade, and the ground between them was dry brown desert.

So where could the cat be? In some coyote's stomach or pecked to pieces by the crows? And what if the car that hit him had hurt him so bad that he was dying? No, she told herself, no, the cat was alive. He was lying somewhere, maybe weak and helpless, but alive and waiting for her.

That evening after dinner, Tess's father drove her back to the old neighborhood for another thorough search. They even rang doorbells where there were lighted windows, but no one had seen a gray and white striped cat with white paws.

They checked the signs Blair had put up, and Dad inked in an offer of a reward for anyone who called their phone number with information. A sliver of moon, set off by a star-filled sky, hung over them by the time they gave up

141

and drove back toward Blair's house. Tess watched the moon sadly, as if it symbolized her waning hope. Still, she slept that night. She was too exhausted not to.

What she had to do was to think like a cat, Tess told herself the next morning on the way to school. Where would she go if she were scared and hurt? Her mother's patio was the only place that came to mind—probably because she *wasn't* a feline, she told herself. No doubt the cat had found a better spot to lick its wounds—or maybe die. If only she had been with him after the car hit him, he would at least have known that she really loved him.

Friday afternoon when Tess got home from school, Blair reluctantly informed her that no one had called in response to the signs. "I'll drive you back there so you can search again, Tess," Blair said, "Although, to be honest, I think—"

"I know. He's dead. But what if he isn't?"

"Yes," Blair's pert face radiated sympathy. "It'd be rotten if he were waiting for us to find him and we didn't."

Blair's understanding surprised Tess enough to make her wonder if she had underestimated her stepmother.

". . . so Mrs. Jackson can watch baby Sara while she's napping, and we'll take Annie and Brian with us," Blair was saying. "Let's go."

This time when she got to her mother's condo, Tess remembered hiding her backpack under the bougainvillea that first day when Mom wasn't home. She'd looked there already, of course, but it was impossible to see all the way to the back, where thin, thorny branches twisted and twined their way up the wall. A tent of space might be left there.

Tess reached around through the brilliant red blooms that Dad had told her were really not flowers but leaves. She forced her bare arm past the thorns, gritting her teeth as they scratched her. Her fingers touched something soft. She yanked her hand back in horror. But the softness had been warm. She got down on her hands and knees. Way at the back, barely visible, was what looked like a dirty rag. Even though he didn't have the strength to resist her, she had a hard time easing the cat out.

"Blair!" she screamed. "Blair, I found him."

Her stepmother came running and cried, "Oh, the poor animal! We'd better get him to a vet. There's one at the corner of Oracle."

"Yuck! Don't put that thing in the car," Brian said.

"Brian, be quiet," Blair said.

Annie was asleep in her car seat. Tess climbed in next to Blair and lowered the cat gently onto her lap. He stirred and made a soft mewling sound, but he didn't open his eyes.

He was still limp and barely breathing when Tess laid him on the cold metal table in the veterinarian's examining room.

"Wait outside with your family, honey. We'll examine him and tell you what's up," the thin blond woman with muscular arms said to Tess.

"I'd rather stay here," Tess said.

The vet shook her head. "Sorry, but we'll do better if you're outside," she said.

Not a good sign, Tess thought. Blair drew Tess out into the waiting room, where Brian and Annie were looking at picture books.

"Can they make him all well?" Annie asked.

"We hope so," Blair said. She looked at Tess, who was chewing on her lip, and said, "At least he's still alive, Tess."

"If he lives, he can't go back to Ria's house. Her father hates him."

"Don't you worry. We'll find him a good family," Blair said.

Strangers, Tess thought with distaste. At least Ria was a friend and she'd shared the cat—not willingly, of course—but still she'd shared him. Tess wondered if Gunther liked only lizards.

It seemed forever until the vet came out and said, "Well, he's in shock and dehydrated. There may be some internal injuries. We should keep him here and see how he does. Why don't you call us in the morning?"

"Is he going to live?" Tess asked.

"I hope so," the vet said. "But there's no way to be sure." She looked Tess in the eye and added, "He's not in very good shape, I'm afraid."

"I want to see him."

The vet looked at Blair, who nodded. "Okay," the vet

said. "You can say good night to him, but only for a minute."

The cat seemed to have melted onto the table, and he gave no sign of life as Tess gently stroked his rumpled fur with the tip of her finger. "Oh, Cat," she said, her eyes filling with tears. "Oh, Cat! We never even got to name you."

Blair took her arm. "Thank the doctor, Tess, and let's go."

"But I want to stay with him," Tess said. "He'll feel better if I'm here."

"Please, don't make a scene," Blair said quietly. "They'll take good care of him for you. You can't stay, Tess. You know you can't."

Reluctantly Tess followed her stepmother out to the car. Annie took her hand, and suddenly Tess picked Annie up and hugged her. It felt good when Annie hugged back hard.

Chapter 16

They went to McDonald's that night. Dad and Blair concentrated on baby Sara, who was being fussy. She kept nursing at the bottle Blair held for her, then rejecting it and crying. While Annie and Brian played in the cage with the big plastic balls and climbed through the tunnels, Tess sipped endlessly at a chocolate milkshake. Blair had suggested it when Tess said she couldn't eat anything. Dad took the baby from Blair and rocked her in his arm. She quieted, but when he tried to give her the bottle, baby Sara screamed.

"Let me try," Tess said.

Blair gave her a funny look and glanced at Dad. He nodded and handed Tess the baby. She laid baby Sara over her shoulder and patted her back, as she had seen Blair do. Whether the moment was right or whether her touch was what was needed, baby Sara gave a big burp. Blair handed Tess the bottle and the baby sucked at it contentedly.

"Well," Dad said with a big grin. "Well, how about that?"

Tess made a face at him and said, "I can do lots of stuff you don't know about, Dad."

"You know," Blair mused, "we always had a cat when I was a child."

"You did? Did you like them?" Tess asked.

"Oh, yes," Blair said. "I love cats."

"Really?" Tess looked at her stepmother as if she'd suddenly sprouted a halo.

"You should have told her that before," Dad said. "Maybe she wouldn't have run away from home."

"If I hadn't gone to live with Mom, I wouldn't have found the cat," Tess said. "Dad, couldn't we build a cage for him in the yard, a big cage? I'd pay for it."

Dad gave her a long look. Then he said, "You know, a guy at work told me his wife had a cat when he married her. He turned out to be allergic to it and she made him get shots."

"So?" Tess said.

"So he says it's not that bad."

"Would you do that for me, Dad? Get shots and let me keep the cat?"

Her father grimaced. "I don't know," he said. "That's a lot to ask. I'd have to take those shots for as long as the cat lives, and that could be years."

"Please, Daddy," Tess said. "He wouldn't be any bother. I'll clean his litter pan and feed him. And he'd be in my room most of the time. He's really a wonderful cat. I mean, he's clean and smart. He scratched Ria's guesthouse door. But any damage he does, I'll pay for out of my allowance." She stopped for breath and looked at her father.

"Let's see if the cat makes it first," he said cautiously.

She thought she could read his mind. He was hoping the cat would die so he wouldn't need to decide just how much he loved his oldest daughter. Bitterly she said, "And what if he lives?"

He sighed. "So what would I get out of keeping him, then?" her father asked, "I mean, besides shots?" He rolled out his lower lip and frowned at her.

He was bargaining, Tess realized. She drew another deep breath, let it out, and said quickly, "If you take the shots, I'll pick up my room. I'll baby-sit Annie and Sara. I'll be so good you won't recognize me."

"Now, that's pretty tempting," Dad said. His frown had turned into a smile.

"And you could name the cat," Tess said. "You could name him anything you like."

Blair and Dad laughed as if Tess had said something funny.

It was hard for Tess to sleep that night. She woke up in the middle of a nightmare about the cat running and being hit with a solid black object. Tears leaked into her pillow as she imagined the cat lying in the hospital in a cage and waking up with no one around to comfort him. She said a prayer for him and made a fervent promise to remake herself in Ria's image if only he lived.

In the morning Tess called the vet's office. The cat was still alive.

Two days later the vet herself got on the phone and said he was getting better. The day after that Tess was told she could come and take him home.

Dad gulped when he saw the hospital bill, but he paid it without comment. The cat lay placidly in Tess's arms on the way back to Blair's house, although he meowed now and then as if to ask where they were going.

"I don't know," Tess answered him. "Dad hasn't said yet."

"Hmm?" Dad asked.

"I told the cat that you hadn't made up your mind about giving him a home."

For an answer Dad sneezed. He made a sour face at the cat and Tess edged closer to her side of the car. Neither she nor her father spoke another word to each other.

When they got back, Blair was making cookies with Brian and Annie.

"Oooh, can I pet him?" Annie asked.

"Sure." Tess knelt and Annie stroked the cat's head with one pudgy finger. He looked up at Tess with black marbles of fear in his eyes, but he hunkered down in her arms and tolerated the petting. "It's all right," she reassured him. "Annie's a sweetie."

"Does he have a name?" Brian asked.

"Just Cat," Tess said. "Whoever gets to keep him will give him a name, I guess."

"That's fair," Blair said. She smiled at Dad.

He nodded and said, "When I was a kid, I wanted to get into motocross racing more than anything, but I could never get enough money together for a bike. Well, I also wanted a pet. So my birthday came and my folks gave me a black and white kitten. I named him Motocross, or Mo for short. . . . He had the biggest purr, bigger than he was. But it didn't take long to find out I was allergic to him. We ended up giving him away."

"Motocross?" Blair asked dubiously. Both her eyebrows went up this time.

"Mo," Dad said. He looked at Tess. "You said I could name the cat if we kept it, didn't you?"

Tess caught her breath, barely able to believe what she had heard.

"Mo's a cool name," Brian said.

"Mo's just the name I've been looking for," Tess said as if she meant it. She was rewarded with a big grin from her father. "Hey, Mo," she addressed her cat, "What do you think of your new name?"

Obligingly the cat bumped his head against her chest

and began a ragged purr that sounded like a car engine in need of a tuneup.

The phone rang. Blair picked it up and murmured, "Fine. She's right here." She handed the receiver to Tess.

"So what's up, Tess? How're you doing with the happy-ever-after family?" Mom asked her.

"We brought the cat home. Dad's letting me keep him."

"You're kidding! Your father said you could keep him? He must really love you."

"Yeah," Tess said. "Dad named the cat Mo."

"Mo? What kind of name is that?" Mom said.

"It's different," Tess said and added firmly, "I like it. . . . What are you doing about that guy you changed the locks for?"

"Oh, I called Haig and told him the police were watching my condo. I said if he ever comes near me, or scares my child again, I'll get Teddy to beat him up. Teddy's got a black belt in karate, among other things."

"You're still seeing Teddy?"

"For now," Mom said. "Why, Tess, don't you like him?"

"He's okay. He's just not—I mean, Dad's a whole lot better."

Mom laughed. "So long as I don't have to live with him, I agree."

"I guess," Tess said judiciously. "I guess *I* can live with him. And Blair. And Annie and Brian, and baby Sara—and Mo."

"Well, good for you," Mom said. "And when you want a break from being perfect, you can come hang out with me. How about this weekend?"

"Mo's not welcome, is he?"

"No, he's not."

"Well, then, not this weekend, Mom. I don't want to leave him alone until he's used to it here."

"You're sounding like your father again. Mr. Responsible."

"So," Tess said. "What's wrong with that?"

"Nothing," Mom said. "I guess you're an okay kid, whoever you take after."

Tess blinked at the compliment. "Thanks," she said, practicing from the rule list Blair had typed up and posted on her closet door. The word fell from her lips more easily than she'd thought it could. As for keeping her room neat, it shouldn't be all that hard. She'd have to start practicing before baby Sara moved in. "Well, goodbye, Mom. Take care," Tess said.

"Tess," Mom said. "Don't forget I love you, too."

"Don't worry, Mom," Tess said cheerfully. "It's mutual."

She hung up and nuzzled Mo who was draped over her shoulder. Delicately he licked her chin in approval. Softly he flicked his tail against her arm. If Tess could have purred in return, she would have. She wondered if Blair would like to have another one of those Home, Sweet

Home signs. The one Tess had ruined had been taken off the wall. Maybe she'd buy one in wood for Mother's Day, or the next time she went to the mall.

Of course, a Home, Sweet Home sign still struck her as icky, but now, at least, the message rang true.